"A ROLLICKING ADVENTURE."

KIRKUS REVIEWS

"A WILD RIDE THAT'S FUN, FREAKY, OUTLANDISH, AND SUSPENSEFUL."

BOOKLIST

"AMAZING AND MIND GLOWING."

FENGYI, AGED 11

"STRANGE BUT GENIUS."

PRITESH, AGED 11

"DO YOU BELIEVE IN MAGIC? DIDN'T THINK SO. AFTER READING THIS BOOK, YOU DEFINITELY WILL!"

THE CITY OF SECRET RIVERS

JACOB SAGER WEINSTEIN

Illustrations by Euan Cook

WALKER
BOOKS

First published in Great Britain 2017 by Walker Books Ltd
87 Vauxhall Walk, London SE11 5HJ

This edition published 2018

2 4 6 8 10 9 7 5 3 1

Text © 2017 Jacob Sager Weinstein
Cover art and illustrations © 2017 Euan Cook
Photograph credits: The Print Collector/Alamy Stock Photo (p.339);
Tim Whitby/London GVs/Alamy Stock Photo (p.340);
Jacek Wojnarowski/Shutterstock (p.341 left);
Tupungato/Shutterstock (p.341 right);
Eric Nathan/Alamy Stock Photo (p.342)

The right of Jacob Sager Weinstein to be identified as author of this
work has been asserted by him in accordance with the
Copyright, Designs and Patents Act 1988

This book has been typeset in Goudy Old Style

Printed and bound by CPI Group (UK) Ltd, Croydon CR0 4YY

British Library Cataloguing in Publication Data:
a catalogue record for this book is available from the British Library

ISBN 978-1-4063-7838-2

www.walker.co.uk

FOR
ERIN AND J

PART
ONE

CHAPTER 1

In 1848, London smelled awful. I'm not sure why this surprised anybody. If I had been around then and somebody had said, "Hyacinth, if every toilet in town flows directly into the river Thames, will the city smell like a rose garden in a chocolate factory?" I'm pretty sure I would have said, "Um, no."

But apparently it was a big surprise to the Victorians. They called it the Great Stink, and at first, all the members of Parliament ignored it. Then the stink reached the Parliament building, and when everybody finished running gagging out of the building, they figured maybe they should do something about it.

They dug up half the city and built a massive underground sewer. They spent huge amounts of money, and they ripped up the road and tore down houses, but they did it in the name of good health and breathable air. It was just a big engineering project, and it had *absolutely nothing* to do with a terrifying magical power that could destroy London and possibly the whole planet if it got into the wrong hands.

At least, that's what the history books told me. But you know what?

History is a big fat liar.

And you know who else is a liar? My mom.

OK, that's not fair. It's only lying if you're clued in enough to know you're not telling the truth. I honestly think Mom believes everything she says, even if it completely contradicts something she said thirty seconds before.

Consider the following Mom Monologue, which I heard as our black cab pulled away from London Heathrow Airport:

"Now, honey, I know you're scared about moving to a new country, and maybe you're a little angry at me, but you're going to fall in love with London, I just *know*. It's a wonderful big city full of exciting things. It'll be totally different from what you're used to, and that will help you grow! Also, Aunt Polly's flat is in Hampstead, which is the part of London where she and I and all your aunts grew up, and it's just beautiful.

There are sheep wandering through fields, and springs welling up between the trees. It'll be like you never left Grandma's farm back in Illinois, and that will help you feel right at home!"

You see what I mean? I counted four contradictory statements in about ten seconds. You would think that one of them, at least, would turn out to be right, but Mom has a rare knack for missing the truth on all sides.

And when we finally got to Hampstead, I realized she'd done it again. It wasn't bustling and exciting, but it wasn't full of sheep and springs, either. It was just an ordinary neighbourhood with some trees and some buses. Aunt Polly's building was on a busy four-lane road, and I'm pretty sure any sheep that tried to wander across it would have ended up as lamb chops. So maybe things had changed since my mom was a little girl ... except the buildings looked like they were at least a hundred years old, which means that my mom couldn't have grown up among open fields unless she was much, much older than she looked.

Still, I was excited about seeing Aunt Polly. A long time before I was born, my mom and her eight sisters had left England and moved to a little town in Illinois, where my grandmother had bought a farm. I had grown up surrounded by family, and since Aunt Polly had moved back to London last year, I'd missed her terribly. Spending time with her was the only part of this whole crazy move that I expected to actually enjoy.

Mom let us into the building with the key Aunt Polly had mailed her, and we lugged our bags up two flights of steps. Then we had to lug them up another flight. "I thought Aunt Polly's flat was on the second floor," I said.

"Oh, here in England, they call… No, I should say, here in England, *we* call the first floor the ground floor. So when we say 'the first floor', that's actually the second floor, and when we say 'the second floor', that's actually the third floor."

Great, I thought. *It's not just Mom. The whole country is lying to me.*

Mom unlocked Aunt Polly's door and swung it open. "Hello, Polly! We're here," she called. There was no answer.

I spotted a note on a nearby table and read it out loud:

Dear Cleo and Hyacinth,
So sorry I can't be there to meet you. One of my companies in Tokyo is on the verge of collapsing, and I've had to fly over there to fix it.

*I'll be back in a month or two.
Until then, please make yourselves
at home.*

Love, (Aunt) Polly.

That was strange, because when it came to being organized, Aunt Polly was kind of the anti-Mom. Even when she had a million different things going on at once (which was usually), Aunt Polly never missed a single detail. Flying off at the last minute was totally unlike her.

It looked like it was going to be just me and Mom for most of the summer. Whoopee.

"That's disappointing," Mom said. "I was really hoping Polly would be around to help me sort out my life. But I was worried we'd be too dependent on her, so I'm glad we have some time to ourselves. I'm sure she'll be back soon, unless she takes a long time to fix her company, which she might, so it will probably be ages. Oh, did I tell you Grandma gave me a present to give you when we arrived? I've got it here somewhere."

I had kind of tuned Mom out, like I usually did when she started on one of her monologues, but that last bit caught my attention. Despite everything, I felt a little tingle of excitement. Grandma always gave the best presents.

I waited impatiently while Mom opened up her suitcase and sorted through all the junk she had packed. Finally, she emerged victorious and handed me a gift-wrapped package.

I ripped open the wrapping and found a book inside: A *History of the Sewers of London*.

Huh. Well, I guess it kind of made sense. Grandma knew I liked history. She knew I was good at plumbing and stuff like that. She knew I was moving to London. I wasn't sure I'd put all those facts together in quite the same way she had, but she'd never given me a bad present, so I was willing to give her the benefit of the doubt.

I opened it up and found she had written something on the front page:

My dearest Hyacinth,
I write this with heavy heart, for you and your mother are heading into

terrible danger you cannot possibly anticipate. I wish I could guide you through it, but you must face it on your own. All I can do is tell you this: your aunts and I have done what we can to prepare you. Remember, my child. As long as you remember, I will always be with you.

With eternal love,

Grandma

Wait, WHAT??? If Grandma knew about real danger, why wouldn't she do something about it? And how had she and my aunts prepared me? They had told me a million random stories, and they had taught me a million random skills, but if I was heading towards terrible danger, knowing how to milk a cow or fix a harpsi-chord wasn't going to do me much good.

I showed the note to Mom and said, "What does *that* mean?"

Mom shrugged. "I think she meant what she said, sweetie. She just wants you to have fun in London."

Puzzled, I looked back down at the page. Grandma's note now said something completely different:

Dear Hyacinth,
Have fun in London!
Love,
Grandma

CHAPTER 2

*T*he first few weeks, the only danger I encountered was the danger of Mom driving me crazy. She tried to show me around, but she kept getting lost, and when we did find a place, whatever she had to tell me was wrong. We spent two hours wandering around the Tower of London, looking for the live lions Mom insisted were kept there, before she finally believed the guards who kept telling her she was thinking of the London Zoo.

Also – and I know it sounds like a small thing, but it drove me crazy – the taps in Aunt Polly's flat made no sense. Back home, every sink had a mixer tap, so that the hot and cold water flowed together and came out at just the right temperature. For some reason, every sink in Aunt Polly's flat had one tap for hot water and another one for cold, so you either burned your skin or froze it.

"You're supposed to put in the plug and then mix the hot and cold water in the sink, sweetie," Mom said when I complained.

"But then gunk from the last person who washed their hands gets in the water."

"It's like Grandma always said," Mom told me. "When your home is in a new place, you have to learn how to wash your face."

I had managed to be patient with Mom the whole time we were in London, but as silly as I knew it was, this was the last straw. I lost it. "OK, first of all, this is *not* my home. Second, Grandma never said anything remotely like that. Third, it doesn't even make sense. And fourth, I'm not five years old. Putting something in rhyme is not going to make me believe it."

"It's not supposed to make you believe it, sweetie. It's supposed to help you remember it."

"Mom, that's not the point. Focus."

Mom took my hand. "I know it's hard for you. But wherever we're together, it's home."

"I'm glad you're holding my hand, Mom. Feel how chapped it is? That's because of the taps."

If I just could have gotten some time with somebody other than Mom, it wouldn't have been so bad. But apparently summer vacation starts later in England, because all the kids my age were still in school. Mom told me I should just hang out near a school and start up conversations with kids as they left, but I'm not exactly the walk-up-to-a-stranger-and-start-talking type.

So the only other person I ended up seeing regularly was our elderly downstairs neighbour. She never introduced herself to me – she just looked at me suspiciously when I passed her in the stairwell. Once, we got some of her mail by accident, and I saw from the address that her name was Lady Roslyn Hill-Haverstock, which seemed impressive. It was a little less impressive when I went downstairs to slip it through her mail slot and she yanked the door open to glare at me and I could smell the alcohol on her breath.

"Have you been stealing my post?" she said.

My grandmother taught me to always be polite to my elders, even when they're drunk and paranoid, so I smiled sweetly and said, "Have a lovely day." She slammed the door on me.

But I must have made a good impression on her, because after that, she was friendlier. She'd stop by and ask if there was anything we needed, and occasionally when Mom and I went out, I'd open our front door and find her there, as if she was just about to knock. (Or as if she was eavesdropping, but I couldn't imagine anybody dying to hear our conversations, unless they were doing some kind of secret documentary on Crazy Things Moms Say.)

Having Lady Roslyn around made the building seem a little less lonely, but I wished it weren't the closest I had come to making a friend since we had moved. Mostly, I sat around our flat, reading and rereading *A History of the Sewers of London*. Maybe the letters would rearrange themselves and I'd learn something about the terrible danger I was in, but they were in the same order every time. I started to think I had just imagined Grandma's warning. It must just have been the stress of the move.

I will give Mom credit for one thing: although she never made much sense on a minute-by-minute basis, things did have a way of working out in the end. One night, she tried to make macaroni and cheese for dinner, but she accidentally flipped over to another recipe halfway through, and she ended up making macaroni and cheese pancakes. I was *not* going to eat those. I sent her out to the grocery store but then decided I'd better go with her, to make sure she bought something sensible. Then she managed to get us lost, plus it turned out that instead of her wallet, she had filled her purse with pancakes.

All of which should have been a disaster, except that we ended up in a huge park called Hampstead Heath, which really was full of those rolling hills and leafy trees she had promised me. And it turns out that when it's summer in London, the sun stays up for ever, which meant that as late as it was, we could sit on a hill and watch the sun set, eating the pancakes she had conveniently brought along. And you know what? Macaroni and cheese pancakes are really good. It ended up being the best night we'd had since we moved.

After a few weeks, things settled into a pattern. I still missed home – no matter what Mom said, I was *not* going to fall in love with London. But at least I was learning to tolerate it.

And maybe Mom was learning to listen to me, because one morning, when she had gone out shopping, a plumber showed up to replace our tap. It was a pretty simple process. He took out the old taps, connected the hot and cold water pipes with one long pipe, and put a new mixer tap on it. Voilà. Done. Easy.

When he had gone, I stood in front of the bathroom sink, turned on the hot and cold taps, took a deep breath, and put my hands in the water.

I stood there, my mouth open, unable to believe what I was feeling. It was true that hot and cold water were both coming out of the same place. But somehow they stayed completely separate. One side of the stream was way too hot, and the other side was way too cold. British engineering had achieved the impossible: it was chapping my hands in two different ways at the same time.

If I had known what the day had in store for me, I would have stood there all morning, no matter how uncomfortable it was. But I didn't know, so I jerked my hands back.

At that moment, the phone rang. It was Dad.

"Hi, my love," he said.

"Hi, Dad! I'm so glad you called. Mom's driving me—" I stopped, because he had taken the kind of deep breath he only takes when he's about to make a big announcement.

For just a moment, my imagination ran wild. He was going to tell me I could come live with him, and we'd both move back to Illinois, and my mom could stay in London! No, even better – he and Mom had realized they made a huge mistake, and they were getting back together, and we were all moving home!

But what he actually said was "Jessica and I are getting married."

CHAPTER 3

"*W*HAT?"

"Well, she and I have been together almost two years, and—"

I shouldn't have interrupted. Or if I did, I should have just said "Congratulations". Or if I couldn't bring myself to say that, at least I should have said something like "Hmm". But what came out of my mouth was "How could you do this to me?"

And then I should have said "Sorry", because that probably wasn't a fair thing to say. But what I actually did was hang up the phone.

My dad called right back. Or at least, I assume he did, because the phone rang again, but I just picked it up and then hung up immediately.

I know, I know. I would absolutely, definitely have handled it much better if my dad had called back a third time, but he didn't, which was probably just because I was acting like I didn't want to talk to him and he was trying to respect that, but right then, I thought it proved he was a jerk who didn't care about me at all.

Fine. I couldn't count on my dad; I couldn't count on my mom; and apparently I couldn't even count on the stupid plumber. But if I couldn't fix all the things my parents had screwed up, I sure as heck *could* fix that stupid sink, and that was EXACTLY what I was going to do.

I stormed into the bathroom and was surprised to see a toolbox sitting on the floor. The plumber must have left it there. I opened up the toolbox, and I got another surprise. There was only one tool inside, and it looked like no tool I had ever seen before. Or, actually, it looked like all the tools I had ever seen, all at once. It looked kind of like a wrench, and kind of like a hammer, and kind of like a shovel, and kind of like a hacksaw.

I picked it up and nearly dropped it, because the moment I touched it, I felt an electric shock shoot down my arm. But the shock went away almost immediately, and when it had gone, I had the most amazing feeling, like the tool was part of my arm and I could do *anything* with it.

I turned off the water to the sink, and in a matter of moments, I had removed the mixer tap. I looked inside it, and there was a little copper tube wedged into the tap. That must have been what kept the hot water and the cold water separate. I tried to pull it out; it wouldn't budge. Then I gave it a tap with the hammer part of the tool, and it popped right out.

It was a normal copper tube, except that it had an odd design etched into it. It looked like a rabbit with a misshapen arm:

Weird. I guessed it was the symbol of whatever company made it. But I didn't particularly care. I threw the copper tube into the trash, reattached the mixer tap with the wrench-hammer-shovel-hacksaw thingy, and switched the water back on. Then I took a deep breath and turned on the taps.

Miracle of miracles, warm water came out. Not hot water. Not freezing water. Not water that was burning hot and freezing cold at the same time. Gentle, soothing, warm water. I closed my eyes and let it wash over me. For one brief moment, something in my life was exactly what it was supposed to be.

Unfortunately, it was a very brief moment, because almost immediately, my hands started to vibrate, like there was a very local earthquake happening only in the sink.

I opened my eyes. Then I yanked my hands back, because instead of water, *fire was pouring out of the tap.*

No, wait. It wasn't fire. It was still water. But it was glowing with an inner flame. As it plunged down into the sink, it twisted and leapt downwards, in the same way a candle flame twists and leaps upwards.

Very, very, very carefully, I reached out and touched it. It didn't burn, but my finger started vibrating again. I pulled my hand back.

I was a little freaked out, but only for ten seconds, because that's how long it took for something *really* freak-worthy to happen. The weird, fiery, vibrating water started to clamber over the edge of the sink like a chimp escaping its cage.

This was not good. Fire burns down buildings. Water floods them. I didn't know which one the fire-water was going to do, but either way, Aunt Polly wasn't going to be happy to come home and find out I had destroyed her flat. Plus, did glowing water mean it was radioactive? Was I downstream from some kind of nuclear meltdown?

I wanted to run out the door screaming, but I couldn't just let this freaky wet hazard keep flowing out and onto the floor. What if I saved myself but the water flooded the whole building and killed everybody else in it? I figured I would give myself one minute to fix it, and if I couldn't, I'd get the heck out of there and let somebody in a radiation suit try instead.

I tried to turn off the taps, but they wouldn't budge. In desperation, I grabbed the wrench-hammer-shovel-hacksaw thing and slammed it into the hot water tap.

The tap whirred around rapidly and shut itself off.

I slammed the tool into the cold water tap, and it whirred around, too. The water was off. Now all I had to do was mop up the puddle on the floor before it leaked down into Lady Roslyn's flat.

Unfortunately, the puddle didn't want to get mopped up. I grabbed one of Aunt Polly's fancy Egyptian cotton towels and threw it onto the floor – *and the water dodged it*. It just slithered over to the left.

OK. I didn't know what was going on, but it was definitely not radiation. Maybe there were microscopic minnows in the water, which would explain why it was a funny colour, and when they darted around, they kind of sploshed the water around. And maybe the tingling was the fish nibbling my skin, like the time Aunt Mel took me to the spa where you put your feet in the water and fish nibbled off the dead skin. Yeah. That was the most logical explanation I could come up with.

I grabbed another towel and threw it at the puddle, which made the puddle jump out of the way again, so I threw another towel, and the puddle dodged that, too, but fortunately, I was smarter than a puddle of water, and I had planned my throws carefully. The water was now trapped between three towels. It seemed to know it, too, since it started trembling nervously, darting helplessly around.

With one last frantic effort, the puddle picked itself up off the floor and tried to jump over the wall of towels I had built. I don't know how a puddle jumps, exactly, but however it did it, it couldn't jump very far. It landed on a towel and got soaked up with a loud *SPLOSH!*

Well, almost all of it did. One single drop managed to spatter over the side. It slid along the floor, then skidded to a stop, stood up for a moment, and turned back towards me. It didn't have eyes, but I swear, somehow I knew it was looking at me. (But no, that was impossible. *It's just little minnows sploshing around*, I reminded myself. *Right?*)

Then the drop turned back the other way, as if it were looking at the wall.

I followed its gaze (or, at least, where its gaze would be, if it weren't a drop of water). It was looking at a crack in the wall. It wasn't a big crack, but it was just big enough for a drop of water to squeeze through.

We stood there for a moment, the drop of water and I.

And then we both leapt at once.

I leapt towards the drop, grabbing one of the towels off the floor as I flew through the air, like an action hero grabbing a gun in the middle of a big shoot-out.

And the water leapt for the crack in the wall.

What happened next felt like it was in slow motion. As I moved closer to the drop, the drop inched closer to its escape route. I was almost there – I stretched out the hand holding the towel – another split second and I'd have it—

—and just before I reached it, it slipped into the crack.

I slammed into the wall and slid down onto the floor.

As I lay there, the bathroom door swung open. But it wasn't my mom. It was our downstairs neighbour, Lady Roslyn. She stared at the towel that had soaked up most of the puddle. It was writhing around like there was a rabid raccoon under it.

The funny thing was, she didn't look baffled at the sight of a wriggling wet towel. She looked *scared*.

"Did any water escape?" she asked.

"No! Not at all! Except for one little drop. Maybe. Definitely."

"You foolish girl," she said. "Do you have any idea what you've just unleashed?"

"Um … minnows?" I said.

CHAPTER 4

*I*gnoring my answer, Lady Roslyn ran over to the sink and examined it. "You mixed hot and cold water?"

"I just didn't want my hands to be chapped," I said, although somehow, saying it out loud made it seem much less reasonable.

"I see," Lady Roslyn said. "And I suppose you thought we English were too simple to have thought of mixing hot and cold water?"

"No! I just thought—"

"Oh, no need for shame. Why should the nation that discovered evolution, produced the works of Shakespeare, and conquered the entire globe be able to master basic bathroom plumbing? Who would imagine that we'd have a very good reason for keeping the hot water separate from the cold?"

"The shower mixes hot and cold water—"

"Exactly!" she said. "And you do your best thinking in the shower, don't you?"

"Um… Yes, I guess…"

She grinned triumphantly, as if she had just proven some incredibly important point. I had no idea what she was talking about, but I felt like I needed to take charge of the conversation, so I said, "And what are you doing in my flat, anyway?"

"When my ceiling started glowing, I thought it best to investigate."

"How'd you get in our front door?"

"Locks are easy, little girl. At least, *mechanical* locks."

"First of all, I'm not a little girl. I'm twelve. Second, all locks are mechanical."

I thought those were both excellent points, but she didn't bother responding to either of them. "Have you had your kettle read recently?"

"My kettle?"

She sighed. "Yes, your kettle. To boil water in? To make tea?"

"Oh! You want to read my tea leaves? I don't—"

"Nonsense," Lady Roslyn said. "Only superstitious

idiots read tea leaves. They change with every cup, don't they?"

"Yes, but—"

"And do you suppose your fate changes that often? Awfully convenient, wouldn't it be? 'Oh, dear, I've just been convicted of murder and I'm about to head to the gallows. Let me just drink a different cup of tea, and suddenly I'll be king of Sweden.' Poppycock. Now, where's your kettle?"

"It's in the kitchen, but—"

Before I could finish the sentence, she had swept out of the room. I followed her into the kitchen, where she picked up the electric kettle on Aunt Polly's counter. She flipped up the lid and peered in. I looked over her shoulder, but there wasn't much to see – just a pattern of white curves on the bottom of the kettle, left behind when the water had been poured out.

At least, that's what I thought it was. To Lady Roslyn, it must have seemed a lot scarier, because when she looked up at me, there was fear in her eyes. "Good God," she murmured. "Sweet God in Heaven, have mercy on us all."

She kept staring at me. Finally, just to break the silence, I said the only thing I could think of, which was "It's not actually *my* teakettle. My aunt is letting us stay."

"I see. And this aunt said you should make yourself

at home when it comes to the walls and the ceilings and the floors and all the furniture and all the plates and everything else except this particular teakettle?"

"Well, no, but—"

"Then it's your teakettle. And you have no idea how much trouble you're in. How much trouble we're *all* in."

"I don't underst—"

"How many rivers are under London?"

I actually knew the answer to this one. "I read that in a history book my grandmother gave me. There are a dozen or so rivers. They used to be above the ground, but—"

"A dozen? Pah. There are nine that matter. And by now, that drop of water you so carelessly lost could be in any one of them. And we are going to have to find it and get it back."

I was getting pretty tired of being interrupted. I decided that my best chance to finish a sentence was to try one that consisted of a single word: "Why?"

"Because if we don't get it back, it will mean the end of civilization. Every one of those rivers is—"

This time, it was Lady Roslyn who got interrupted, because somebody started knocking loudly on the front door. Whoever it was called out, "Postman. Sign for a parcel?"

Well, actually, they said, "Possssssssstman. Sssss-sign for a parssssel?" I thought the way they stretched out the Ss was a little weird – but Lady Roslyn seemed to find it much worse. She looked even more terrified.

"The Saltpetre Men!" she cried out. "They've found us already. We'll have to run."

I tried to stay calm. After all, this was a woman who'd just been frightened by a teakettle. I did not exactly have full confidence in her risk-assessment skills.

There was another loud knock on the door, which made us both jump. "Possssssssstman. Sssssssign for a parssssel?"

Lady Roslyn shook her head frantically. I hesitated. Should I listen to her?

But then she said, "Where does your mother keep her cleaning supplies?" and when I pointed under the sink, she pulled open the cabinet there and started rummaging through it frantically.

OK, I thought. *Question answered. She's crazy.*

I went to the front door and opened it.

And I immediately wished I hadn't.

Standing in the hallway was a shambling, stinking monstrosity. It was wearing the red uniform the postman usually wore, but there wasn't much else human about it. It must have been seven feet tall. It had a perfect red circle running all the way around its bald head, but other than that, its skin was lumpy and pale grey with white droppings that looked like bird poop. In place of eyes, it had two bits of glittering rock, like the mica chips my aunt Rainey had once given me.

The whole thing looked like somebody had dug up the dirt underneath a pigeon-filled tree and poured it into a Royal Mail uniform and brought it to life and aimed it at me.

When Grandma's words had changed in the book she'd given me, I'd figured it was just my memory playing tricks. When a glowing drop of water ran away from me, I'd convinced myself it was just radioactive minnows. But there was no scientific explanation possible for this mushy, smelly monster. It was *magic*. That meant everything I had believed about how the world worked was wrong.

I stumbled back in horror. The monster took a step forwards and lifted up its arm, which bent in a bunch of places no arm should ever bend. For a moment, I thought it was going to grab me, and I held up my hands to protect myself—

—but it just held out a clipboard. "Ssssssssignature, pleassse," it burbled.

Since my hands were already up, I took the clipboard. There was an old-fashioned parchment attached to it, with an elegantly calligraphed message:

I, Hyacinth Hayward, do hereby pledge to return the lost drop of water to the nearest Royal Mail office by midnight, on pain of death. (Visit our website to find a Royal Mail office conveniently near you!)

Since the clipboard was the only weapon I had at hand, I threw it at the Saltpetre Man. A corner of it sank into the monster's forehead and just stayed there. The Saltpetre Man didn't seem to notice. "Sssssssignature, pleasssssse."

Wait. Was there an echo in the hall? I craned my head to the side, looking past the monster's bulk.

It was no echo. There were a dozen other Saltpetre Men behind it, all burbling, "Sssssignature, pleassssse."

Run, I thought, but my legs wouldn't move.

"Have no fear," whispered Lady Roslyn's voice in my ear. "There are only two things that can hurt a Saltpetre Man, and one of them is ammonia."

I got control of my muscles enough to turn my head and look back at her. She was clutching a bottle of window cleaner. With a gleeful cackle, she pointed at the closest creature and squeezed the trigger frantically, filling the air with mist.

Nothing happened.

I tried to talk, but no words came out. All I could do was point a trembling finger at the little label on the environmentally friendly window cleaner Mom insisted on buying: MADE WITH PLANT-BASED CLEANERS. AMMONIA-FREE!

Finally, I got a word out. And that word was "RUN!!!"

I ducked under the Saltpetre Man's arm. He swatted at me, but he moved so slowly that I could dodge him. Behind him, the others started bunching together to block me, but they were slow enough that I managed to dive between them.

As I did, I brushed against one of their legs and shuddered. It was slimy, but with a weird warmth. I was so freaked out that I stumbled a little, which gave it enough time to reach down and grab my arm. Its touch was wet and slippery and muddy, and when I jerked my hand back, its fingers crumbled slightly around the edges, which was absolutely disgusting, but it let me break free.

I caught my balance and ran down the steps, with Lady Roslyn close behind me.

We made it to the foyer and out the door and we

were half a block away before they even lumbered out of the building.

I stood there, bent over, trying to catch my breath. When I straightened up, I noticed that Lady Roslyn didn't even seem winded. That was a little weird, but it wasn't even in the top ten weirdest things that had happened to me that day.

Fortunately, it seemed like we could both outrun the Saltpetre Men, whatever they were, so everything was going to be OK. We'd just run a few more blocks and lose them, and then I'd forget I had ever seen glowing water, and everything would be back to normal.

As I was thinking that, a cab pulled up in front of our building. Mom got out. Instead of noticing the gigantic mud monsters standing three feet behind her, she noticed me and waved cheerfully.

"MOM!" I yelled, running towards her. "Watch out for—"

"Mrrrghmrrgh," Mom said as one of the monsters clamped a crumbling hand over her mouth. She struggled frantically, but she might as well have been wrestling a mountain. The Saltpetre Man picked her up and threw her into the back of a Royal Mail van that had parked nearby, as the other Saltpetre Men climbed into the front.

I reached the van just as it pulled away. The

Saltpetre Man who was driving leaned out of the window as the van passed by. "Midnight tonight," it burbled as it threw something small and shiny at my feet: an antique-looking penny. "Midnight tonight," it burbled again.

I got a quick glimpse of my mom's terrified face pressed up again the rear window. And then the van was gone.

I whipped out my phone and dialled 999, which is British for 911.

"Emergency operator," said the emergency operator.

"My mother has been kidnapped by monsters!" I yelled.

As soon as the words were out of my mouth, I realized how crazy they must sound. But the emergency operator was surprisingly matter-of-fact. "Are those monsters in Royal Mail uniforms, or unidentified other monsters?"

"Royal Mail," I said.

"Did they state clearly for you the conditions, magical or otherwise, required for your mother's return?"

"Yes, I guess so, but—"

"Then they're acting within the law, ma'am. Please reserve 999 for genuine emergencies." She hung up.

I stared at the phone for a moment, then dialled my dad, my grandma, and all eight of my aunts. Nobody picked up, which was kind of creepy. Mom and her sisters were constantly calling each other at all hours to solve some crisis or just to chat, and I couldn't remember anybody ever taking more than two rings to answer.

Then I thought about what Grandma's note had said, the first time I had read it: *I write this with heavy heart, for you and your mother are heading into terrible danger you cannot possibly anticipate. I wish I could guide you through it, but you must face it on your own. All I can do is tell you this: your aunts and I have done what we can to prepare you. Remember, my child. As long as you remember, I will always be with you.*

Well, I was remembering, all right, so I guess she was with me in spirit. But honestly, I kind of would rather have had her with me in reality.

I lowered my phone and looked up to find Lady Roslyn tapping her fingers impatiently against her arm. She knelt down, picked up the penny, and handed it to me. "If you're quite finished wasting time," she said, "perhaps we should go and find that drop of water."

CHAPTER 5

"Tell me again why I'm buying an umbrella," I said.

I was inside the news stand at the Hampstead Tube station, waiting impatiently while Lady Roslyn looked slowly through a collection of cheap black umbrellas. They all looked alike to me, but she was lifting each one out of the stand and scrutinizing it carefully.

"Because you failed to bring one with you when you left the flat," Lady Roslyn answered.

"I was being *chased by monsters*. The same monsters who are *holding my mother hostage* while we are shopping for rain gear."

Lady Roslyn handed one of the umbrellas to the man behind the counter. "She'll take this one."

"No, I won't."

"Don't you have any money? I noticed you have a wallet in your pocket. It makes you look rather man-like, but in this particular circumstance, the utility of it nearly makes up for its unattractiveness."

"You noticed I have a wallet? That's great. Have you noticed that I don't have a mother?"

I was trying to stay calm, but my jaw hurt from holding back tears. All I could think of was Mom in the clutches of those gross creatures. Maybe I wasn't sounding as tough as I wanted to, because Lady Roslyn looked carefully at me for a moment, and when she spoke next, she sounded almost sympathetic. "I promise: I have a plan to address that. It requires an umbrella, and it will only work if the umbrella is yours – purchase, payment, and parcel. It may seem indirect, but it's the fastest way to get that drop of water back. And getting that drop of water back is the only way I can think of to get your mother. Buy it, and while we're on our way, I'll explain as much as I can."

I bought it. Five pounds seemed like a pretty small price to pay for an explanation.

We got our tickets, took the long elevator ride down, and found a quiet spot in the Tube carriage. When we were seated and Lady Roslyn had looked around and assured herself that nobody was in earshot, she took a deep breath and began.

"You said you read a history book. Did it tell you why the Romans built London on this particular spot?"

"It was the rivers. Rivers were really important for cities – they were like highways, but for boats."

"Lies! All lies!" Lady Roslyn yelled, so loudly that people at the other end of the carriage looked up at us. She dropped her voice. "The rivers weren't important because you could sail on them. They were important because they were *magic*. Once they arrived at the Thames, they all mixed together and their powers got muddied and diluted. But if you accessed them before that point, and if you knew what you were doing, you could tap into that power for your own ends."

"How?" I asked.

"It depends on what effect you wanted to achieve. You could draw river water and say certain words over it and transform it into a potion that would drive your enemies mad. You could drink it in combination with certain other substances and receive superhuman inspiration. You could wear certain clothes and go swimming at certain hours, and when you reached the riverbank, you could keep swimming, straight up into the air.

"Over time, certain families became particularly

proficient in these techniques. (And when I say 'over time', understand, I'm referring to *centuries*, not decades, or whatever passes for time in your country.) With each generation, a mother – or, more rarely, a father – would pass on the knowledge her family had acquired over hundreds or even thousands of years.

"She would also pass on a code of ethics, because if one has access to an ancient, unstoppable power, it's rather important that there be things one simply won't do."

While she was talking, Lady Roslyn had taken a navy-blue ribbon out of her hair and was tying it around the handle of my umbrella. This seemed like an odd thing to do, but it wasn't exactly the most urgent mystery at the moment, so I just let her keep talking. "Of course, not everybody was happy with this arrangement. Certain selfish individuals wanted the river magic for themselves – individuals who did not share the same family code of ethics. We thought – and yes, I said *we*, meaning myself and my ancestors, for I'm proud to say my family has been on the right side of this battle for millennia – we thought these selfish individuals were the biggest threat to the safety of the nation and the world.

"We were, alas, quite wrong. Unbeknownst to us, a cult had sprung up in secret. They believed there was a way to unleash the rivers, so that every man, woman, and child who so much as touched a single drop could have access to the greatest magical force in history. It would be the equivalent of handing out nuclear bombs as though they were free newspapers. Civilization could not possibly survive. Yet this cult, for reasons I cannot begin to fathom, thought it would be a good thing.

"And they began to recruit allies. Powerful allies. And eventually, their presence led to disaster. You have, perhaps, heard of the Great Fire of London?"

"Sure," I said, happy to have a chance to show Lady Roslyn how much I knew. "It was in 1666. There was a baker who left his oven on all night, and—"

"Wrong," she said. "It was indeed in 1666, and it burned for five days, and it destroyed the entire city. And at its height, with the heat of ten thousand burning roofs scorching the air and the light of ten thousand burning houses searing the eyes and the angry roar of a hundred thousand crackling timbers assaulting the ears, it was very much like Hell. And it's true that a baker started it, but it wasn't because he baked bread."

"Then what did he do?"

"He mixed hot and cold water."

My stomach dropped. Suddenly, Mom wasn't the only person I was worried about.

CHAPTER 6

"Ah, here we are," Lady Roslyn said. "Time to change lines."

As we left the train, I got my voice back. "But—" I began, but Lady Roslyn pointed to the crowds around us and held a finger to her lips.

When we were once more alone, at one end of a Circle line train, I tried again. "But if that's all it takes to activate the magic, why isn't the city always burning down? I've seen plenty of other buildings here where the water comes out of one tap."

"Those buildings aren't above one of the secret rivers. Our building is, which is why I live there. *Somebody* has to be on guard against this sort of catastrophe. Although, even without my presence, there are supposed to be certain safeguards. The idea that a child such as yourself could replace the tap, let alone turn the handles afterwards – it's preposterous. Very few people would believe it."

"Why could I do it?"

Once again, she looked at me with genuine sympathy. "I think it best if I don't answer that. A little knowledge is a dangerous thing, and you seem to be rather a dangerous girl already. Ask me something else."

I didn't even know where to begin. But if I was going to undo the mess I had created, I should probably know how to stop whatever weird, wet magic I had unleashed. "You said there were safeguards. Like, things that could hold the magic back?"

She nodded. "Certain runes, for example… You do know what a rune is, don't you?"

"Umm," I said impressively.

"A rune is a shape with protective magical powers. Like this one." She reached into the neck of her blouse and lifted up a gold pendant on a simple chain. It was a familiar shape:

"That's the zombie bunny rabbit I saw inside the tap!"

For once, Lady Roslyn was speechless. It didn't last long. "That is *not* a zombie bunny rabbit. It is the silhouette of the very first crude clay urn ever fashioned, as sketched on a cave wall at the very moment when humanity first gained some control over water. It is older than any alphabet, and its power helps us restrain the force of magical rivers."

I still thought it looked like a zombie bunny rabbit. While I was debating whether to say that out loud, Lady Roslyn kept going. "And you have seen it many places other than that faucet you vivisected. You have seen it hundreds of times over the course of your life, if not thousands."

OK, now she was just messing with me. "I think I'd remember a shape if I'd seen it a thousand times."

"Yes," Lady Roslyn said. "I would think so, too. Well, here we are. Baker Street."

We stepped out onto the platform, and I headed for the exit. But Lady Roslyn just stood there, looking at me expectantly. "What?" I asked her.

She didn't answer.

"Fine," I said. "Be that way."

I turned back towards the exit, and then I stopped, because I had just realized something incredible.

Every single wall of Baker Street station was covered with the zombie bunny – I mean, the urn rune. There were hundreds of them. *Thousands* of them – big versions on big tiles, and little versions on little tiles, and even big versions of the rune that when you got close enough turned out to be made up of dozens of little versions. I had been through this station a half dozen times since we had moved, and I had never noticed them.

That didn't make me quite as stupid as you might think, though. The runes on the wall were all upside down. And when they were upside down, they didn't look like an urn, or even like a zombie bunny. They looked like this:

"That's Sherlock Holmes!" I gasped.

"No," Lady Roslyn said. "That's a magical rune. I told you that my family has been involved in this fight for centuries. More than a hundred years ago, during the excavations for this station, an ancient society called the Inheritors of Order discovered that Baker Street was the most dangerous magical nexus in London.

They realized that this area would eventually have to be covered in runes to prevent a tremendous catastrophe. But of course, they couldn't simply announce that to the public. So they called upon my second cousin three times removed, Sir Arthur Conan Doyle. Sir Arthur used his literary skills to invent a character who looked exactly like an upside-down urn, and then he wrote a series of adventures about him so gripping that his fame spread around the world, all so that one day, the Inheritors of Order could cover Baker Street with magical protection. Oh, but don't worry. If he were alive today, I'm sure Sir Arthur Conan Doyle wouldn't mind you undoing his life's work just because you wanted to wash your hands in tepid water. I'm sure he'd be overjoyed! 'Hyacinth,' he'd say. 'Don't you worry about civilization. You just cleanse your hands in a fashion slightly less likely to lead to dry skin.'"

"I'm sorry I put civilization in danger. Can you just tell me what to do?"

"First, we're going to the lost property office."

"Why?"

"Because you've lost your umbrella."

She was right. I had been so busy worrying about saving my mom and the world that I hadn't paid any attention to my umbrella. Now it was gone.

CHAPTER 7

$\mathcal{T}$he good news was, the London Underground Lost Property Office was right next to Baker Street station. The bad news was, there was a line.

"The fate of the world is at stake," I said as we stood there. "Is this really the best use of our time?"

"That is *precisely* what this is. What does an umbrella do?"

"Um – it keeps the rain off your head."

"That's right. It controls water."

OK, this was starting to make a little more sense. "Are you saying it's another incredibly powerful rune?"

"A rune is something written, so no. But individual umbrellas do have a small amount of power. Every year, seven thousand umbrellas pass through the Lost

Property Office. And my goodness, what a coincidence, the Lost Property Office just happens to be located above the single most powerful magical nexus. But of course it isn't a coincidence; the Inheritors of Order planned it that way. Every umbrella that comes through here leaves recharged, thereby offering Londoners just a bit of extra protection from stray magical forces. And if that umbrella happens to be lost at exactly the right spot on the Circle line, it gains an extra power, which is going to prove very useful to us. But that power belongs to the owner of the umbrella; claiming somebody else's will do you no good whatsoever, which is why you had to be the one to purchase it."

The line had moved faster than I thought it would. We were already at the Formica counter, where a clerk stood.

"We have lost an umbrella," Lady Roslyn told him.

"You're in the right place," the clerk said. "We've got thousands of umbrellas."

"I'm sure you do," Lady Roslyn replied. "Fortunately, with remarkable foresight, we tied a navy-blue ribbon around the base, precisely so we could identify it if the need arose."

The clerk vanished into the back for a moment and came back with my umbrella, complete with Lady Roslyn's ribbon. "Here you go. Stay dry, now."

Staying dry didn't seem too hard, since it wasn't raining outside. In fact, I still wasn't clear why I even needed an umbrella. "How am I supposed to use this to control water if it isn't raining?"

Instead of answering, Lady Roslyn led me out of the Lost Property Office and to a shopping arcade about a block away. There was a long walkway with shops on either side and a glass ceiling arching high above. The shops themselves had curved glass windows and lots of elaborate wood carvings. It would have been tremendously elegant if it hadn't been covered with dust and in bad need of repainting. It didn't help that every shop was selling the same plastic double-decker buses and Prince Harry posters.

And yet, standing at the street entrance was some sort of caretaker wearing an immaculate Edwardian suit and top hat, like he expected a baroness to swoop up at any moment in a horse-drawn carriage, looking for fine leather gloves.

There was an old wooden sign next to him. Lady Roslyn pointed to the fading words on it:

FOR THE CONVENIENCE OF ALL OUR PATRONS, BAKER ARCADE ASK THAT YOU OBSERVE THE FOLLOWING BYLAWS:

1. There shall be no whistling.
2. There shall be no running.
3. Under NO circumstances shall there be ANY opening of umbrellas WHATSOEVER.

We walked down to the far end of the arcade, away from where the fancy caretaker stood guard. Lady Roslyn said, "The Tyburn, which is one of London's magical underground rivers, starts under the building where you and I live. From there, it runs below Regent's Park, then under Baker Street. It gets faster and more powerful as it goes. It also gets wider. Near this spot is the first place where it is large enough for humans to pass, and there is an entrance. But the entrance has certain magical safeguards. Non-mechanical locks, you might call them. To overcome them, we shall need to—"

"Whistle, run, and open an umbrella?" I said.

Lady Roslyn raised her eyebrows, and I didn't know what made me more proud: that I had finally managed to interrupt Lady Roslyn instead of the other way around, or that she actually looked impressed by what I had said.

"Precisely," she said. "Why don't you try doing one of those things?"

I lifted up my umbrella – but before I could open

it, the caretaker was somehow by my side. I would have sworn he was all the way down at the other end of the arcade, but now here he was, with his hand holding my wrist. "Terribly sorry, miss," he said. "I'm afraid I'll have to ask you not to contravene our clearly posted by-laws."

"Oh, sure," I said. I watched him walk away. This time, I made absolutely sure he was all the way down at the other side, and then I opened the umbrella—

—Or, at least, I *tried to*, because he was somehow right back next to me, his hand closed firmly over the umbrella. I gave him an innocent smile. He squinted at me suspiciously, then headed away again.

"Well tried," Lady Roslyn said, "but we shan't succeed as long as he's here. Now, watch this."

Lady Roslyn opened her eyes so wide that I worried they'd come rolling out, and she pointed them at the caretaker's back, like a pirate aiming a cannon at an enemy ship.

There were tarnished mirrors along the wall, and I could see the caretaker's reflection in them as he walked away. As her glare burned into the back of his head, he started looking a little nervous, and then a lot nervous, and then plain scared. I'll give him credit – even when he got up to terror, he didn't break the clearly posted by-laws against running. He just walked really, really fast. It was only when his feet hit the pavement outside that he broke into a run, screaming as he went.

"How'd you do that?" I asked.

She shrugged. "If one lives long enough, one learns a handful of tricks."

"Why didn't you do it to the Saltpetre Men?"

"It only works on things with brains. Now, then. It's best if you whistle something with personal meaning. A favourite childhood tune, perhaps?"

I opened my umbrella. This time, nobody stopped me. "There's a lullaby my aunts used to sing to me."

"That will do nicely." Lady Roslyn took my hand. "On the count of three, we'll run. Start whistling. And don't forget to close the umbrella just before we jump into the manhole, or it won't fit through."

"Wait, what manhole? Why are we jumping into a manhole?"

"How else do you think we're getting into the sewer?"

"You didn't say anything about sewers."

She snorted. "I said 'powerful rivers that flow under the city.' Do you know anything else that meets that description?"

"But—"

"One! Two! Three! Whistle!" She started running.

I didn't really feel like I had all the information I needed before I jumped into an allegedly magical sewer. But given how tightly Lady Roslyn was holding my hand, I could either get pulled forwards onto my face or start running.

And once I started running, there was no reason not to start whistling.

I'm not going to claim this was the greatest whistling performance in the history of music, because it turns out that whistling while you run is kind of a challenge, even if you aren't carrying an umbrella in one hand and being dragged by a freakishly strong old lady with the other. But even so, just whistling that lullaby was enough to bring back one of my earliest memories.

We were at a family reunion Grandma had hosted, back when Mom and Dad were still happy together. I couldn't have been more than two, and I was supposed to be upstairs in bed, but I could hear everybody laughing from downstairs. I snuck down, and Aunt Uta spotted me lurking just outside the living room. She scooped me up and carried me back upstairs, singing as she went. I was asleep before we even got to my bed.

And now, as scared and confused as I was, whistling the tune filled me with a happiness I hadn't felt in a long time. If I didn't know better, I would have sworn the glow was even spilling out of me, making the grey and dusty arcade seem bright. For a moment, out of the corner of my eyes, I even thought I saw Grandma reflected in one of the dirty mirrors, but I was already running faster and faster and everything was blurring together. I would have expected the umbrella to catch the air and slow me down, but it felt like it was pushing me forwards.

Just at the edge of the arcade, at the spot where it met the pavement, there was a soot-covered Victorian drinking fountain. It obviously hadn't been working for years, but now I could see a little stream beginning to burble up from it. It was half-hearted at first, but as we got closer and closer, the stream got higher and higher, until it was spraying up into the air and splattering down onto the pavement, where it landed on a dusty iron manhole cover.

The water washed away the dirt … and then, somehow, it washed away the cover, too. Below it was only blackness.

And now we were nearly on top of it. Lady Roslyn let go of my hand and jumped into the air, so I jumped, too. Then I remembered the umbrella and somehow manage to shut it in mid-leap.

Lady Roslyn vanished into the manhole, and I went right behind her.

As I dropped, my mom's words flashed through my mind: *Wherever we're together, it's home.* I was finally on my way to get Mom back, and in some strange way, it felt like I was going home.

CHAPTER 8

$\mathcal{A}$nd then I landed in the sewers. It turned out it wasn't like coming home at all, because I had never lived in an old brick tunnel with an ankle-high river of poop flowing along the floor.

As I hit the ground, I almost stumbled over face-first, but I managed to get my balance at the last moment. This was a good thing. It was bad enough landing feet-first in sewage. I didn't want to even think about landing face-first.

Unfortunately, as I stumbled, waving my arms, my phone fell out of my pocket. I reached down to grab it, and I grabbed something else about the same size and shape but much squishier. By the time I was done yelling "EWWWW!" and throwing the squishy thing away and wiping my hands on the least-disgusting-looking part of the brick walls, my phone was long gone.

Darn. It hadn't actually done me much good today, but it felt like my last link to the real twenty-first-century world, where things were powered by batteries instead of ancient mysterious forces.

And now here I was, underground, and cut off from the world above.

The smell was – well, have you ever opened up a nappy bin? Now imagine the baby had diarrhoea. And that it was a baby elephant. That's pretty much what we're talking about. But I didn't actually mind the smell too much, because I had plenty of experience helping Grandma muck out her horses' stalls.

Of course, when we went mucking, Grandma always gave me some warning, and I had time to put on rubber gloves and thick rubber boots. Right now, I was wearing jeans and trainers, and moments after landing, I could feel the sewage soaking through into my socks and squelching between my toes. I could also feel a little bump every time something floated into the back of my leg, which was often. Way too often.

Lady Roslyn, I noticed, had managed to land on the side of the tunnel instead of the middle. Since the tunnel was shaped like an upside-down egg, the ground was curved, which let Lady Roslyn stand above the flow, on dry brick. I quickly stepped up next to her.

My feet were still soaked, but at least there wasn't anything unspeakable bumping into me, so I could bear to look around and see where we were. It was a long brick tunnel, stretching off in both directions as far as I could see. Also as far as I could see, there were those little lumps floating in the dark, swirling, stinking water.

Above us, the manhole cover somehow resealed itself, shutting out the daylight and leaving us in near-total darkness.

"'Underground river' seems like kind of a charitable description," I said.

"Open your umbrella," Lady Roslyn told me.

I did, and then I gasped. It was like the umbrella cast a reverse shadow. Everything that wasn't under the umbrella was still dark — but a beautiful golden light poured down on everything below the umbrella, transforming whatever it touched. As soon as they floated into the glowing circle, the little lumps of grossness transformed into wriggling silver fish, swimming happily through a little slice of clear, clean river, then changing back to brown lumps as soon as they slipped out of the light. One of my feet was outside the circle, standing on crumbling Victorian bricks; the other foot was inside the circle, sinking into the grassy mud of a river's bank.

"Which side is real?" I asked.

"They both are," Lady Roslyn answered. "You are standing on the banks of the river Tyburn, which has flowed through London since time immemorial, and you are standing in the King's Scholars' Pond Sewer, which was built by..." She squinted at the embossed lettering on a nearby brick. "The Metropolitan Board of Works, 1861."

"But the water in our flat didn't taste like either of those. It definitely wasn't sewage, and I'm pretty sure it wasn't river water, either."

"Of course not," Lady Roslyn said. "The anarchist cult I told you about would love to have water flow straight from the rivers into every tap, but nobody else is so foolish. You were drinking the same tap water as everybody else in London. But to reach our building, the pipes that carry that tap water must pass directly above the Tyburn, and that is enough to give them a magical charge."

Lady Roslyn took the navy-blue ribbon from the handle of the umbrella and used it to tie up her long grey hair. "One doesn't want one's hair brushing against the walls here, if one can help it," she said.

I nodded. I had never been more glad that I kept my hair cropped short.

"Now," Lady Roslyn continued, "do you feel a pull in either direction? Does one way or the other feel like the right way to go?"

I wasn't sure what she meant, but I closed my eyes and concentrated. The only way I really wanted to go was back up onto the street, and then straight into the shower, but I was pretty sure that wasn't an option.

I opened my eyes. "I'm sorry."

"No matter. There are other methods. Hold the umbrella open above your head, but hold it loosely. With your free hand, spin the handle."

I tried it. The umbrella spun around and around like a roulette wheel. When it slowed to a stop, the curved bit at the end of the handle was pointing to the wall. And then, all by itself, it turned just a little more, pointing downstream.

"I was afraid of that," Lady Roslyn said. "The drop is heading towards the mouth of the Tyburn. When it has traversed the entire river, the Tyburn's powers will be fully activated."

"And then?"

"And then, Hyacinth, your mother will be far from the only casualty of the day."

She walked off in the direction the handle had pointed. I followed her.

I don't know how long we walked like that, picking our way in careful silence along the sewer/riverbank. Without my phone, and with no way of seeing the sky, it was hard to tell what time it was. As we walked on and the tunnel got wider and deeper, the manholes got higher and higher above our heads.

Occasionally, we'd come to a place where other tunnels dumped their own smelly water into the stream we were following. Every time, I'd spin the umbrella, and it would point in the same direction we'd been going: onwards, where the river got wider and swifter. Every time, Lady Roslyn would shake her head and mutter "Tsk," in a worried way.

Sometimes, a bird would appear on one side in the umbrella's enchanted circle of light and dart across to the other, where it would vanish. Sometimes it would just be part of a bird – a phantom wing beating in mid-air, while the rest of the bird stayed invisible on the other side of the magical divide. Once I even saw a sheep's ear wobble by. But except for those little moments, the novelty of carrying a portable circle of riverbed with me was starting to wear a little thin. If you've seen one disembodied magical floating sheep's ear, you've seen them all.

On the plus side, the sewer was surprisingly pretty, if you ignored the sewage. The tunnel was gracefully curved, and the little stinking tributaries tumbled in through handsome arches. Rusting iron rings were embedded in the brick walls at intervals, at shoulder height. They looked like the ring Aunt Callie had tied her boat to at her cabin on Lake Erie. Did the sewer ever flood enough to ride boats through? What if it happened while we were walking through it?

Eventually, I noticed that the umbrella was starting to quiver. The next intersection we came to, when I spun the umbrella around, the handle pointed forwards so eagerly that it seemed to be jumping out of my hand. I squinted ahead to see what it was reaching for, and I thought I could see a little patch of light way off in the distance. It couldn't be from a manhole cover, because it was coming from the bottom and shining up.

Lady Roslyn and I came to the same conclusion. "I believe that's our drop," she whispered, and started tiptoeing. I wasn't quite sure why she was being quiet – could a drop of water hear us? At that point, anything was possible. I tiptoed, too.

It turned out I shouldn't have bothered. As we got closer to the patch of light, we could hear a rumble getting louder and louder, and by the time we reached the end of our tunnel, the rumble was a roar.

We stood and looked into a huge cavern below us. It was like the Grand Canyon of sewage. Stinky rivers from a dozen other tunnels waterfalled into a vast brick canyon filled with a glowing lake of gross. Last time I had seen it, the drop had glowed, but not brightly enough to light up a whole lake. It must have gotten more powerful since then.

Lady Roslyn started climbing downwards. There was no ladder, but there were plenty of bricks sticking out, and she used those for hand- and footholds. I folded up the umbrella, hooked it over my arm, and followed her.

It wasn't as easy as she made it look. The air was full of mist churned up by all those waterfalls, which made the bricks wet and slippery. And we were high up enough that if I fell into the lake and it wasn't deep enough, I might break my neck. And if it *was* deep enough, I might get swept under by the same waterfalls whose mists were making it hard for me to keep my panicky, white-knuckle grip on the crumbling bricks.

Thanks a lot, waterfalls.

Bit by bit, handhold by handhold, carefully lowered foot by carefully lowered foot, I made it nearly to the bottom.

It was almost time to go into the foul lake. Fortunately, I had a magic tool that could transform at least part of it into lovely clean water. So I opened the umbrella. As soon as I did, light spilled out from it, and when it landed on the bricks I was standing on, they transformed, too. Specifically, they transformed into thin air. I plunged down.

Fortunately, the water wasn't deep there. Unfortunately, it was *cold*.

Lady Roslyn had been just outside the umbrella's lit circle, so her footholds were still there. She leapt down, right next to me. She scooted over and put her arm around me. "If you don't mind, I'd rather be in river water than the sewer water."

I nodded, and together we plunged forwards, towards the glow at the centre of the pool. In a few steps, the water was up to our waists. It didn't get any higher, but the swirling currents and the mossy rocks beneath our feet made it hard to walk. We leaned against each other and picked our way carefully along, until we could see the drop of water, visible as a single, brightly glowing point of light under the surface.

Lady Roslyn pointed at it, and then to my umbrella, and then she mimed a scooping motion. I guess she was miming instead of talking because she didn't want to startle the drop – but unfortunately, as she was doing it, her hand splashed into the water. The glowing point of light darted away.

I swung my umbrella at it and almost caught it, but it was too fast.

Now that the umbrella wasn't over my head, I was once again standing in stinky sewage, but there was no time to think about that. I sloshed after the light. It dodged left, and then right, and then I nearly had it, and then it dodged the umbrella again. This time, it shot directly under the outtake hole where the water poured into a big black pipe leading who-knows-where. The drop must have gotten trapped in the current there, because it started darting back and forth in a frantic circle, trying to leap up into that pipe, but not quite managing it.

I stopped, aimed the umbrella carefully, and scooped it up.

"Marvellous girl!" Lady Roslyn cried, and slapped me on the back.

Bad idea.

It turns out that when you're in the middle of a churning lake of sewage with a slippery floor, slapping someone on the back is one thing you should definitely *not* do.

I started to topple over. Lady Roslyn reached for my arm, but she missed and grabbed the umbrella instead, twisting it out of my hand and making me lose my balance completely.

For a moment, we looked at each other in horror.

And then the current swept me away, straight into the outtake hole.

CHAPTER 9

The dark roared, and the bricks scraped my butt just hard enough to hurt but not hard enough to slow me down, and the twisting tunnel flipped me face down into the sewage, and then face up again just long enough for me to take three desperate gasps before it flipped me down again and then up and then down, and I gasped at the wrong time and ended up sucking foul water into my lungs instead of air, and then I slammed into a brick sticking out. It hurt like heck but at least it sent me spinning face up so I could suck in a smelly, humid gasp of air, and still sliding downwards, and still scraping my butt, and still gasping, and still downwards, and still downwards.

And then, up ahead, a tiny pinprick of light, which

was suddenly as big as a Hula Hoop, and I got sprayed out into another cavern, and I hung in the air for a moment before I plopped down into an even bigger lake of sewage.

I plunged downwards through the disgusting water. My feet scraped the bottom. I pushed off as hard as I could and swam up, my lungs bursting.

And finally, with a gasp, I broke the surface and sucked in breath until my chest stopped feeling like it was about to explode.

Closer to me, just above the water, I saw a little concrete shelf. Maybe it was meant for sewer workers to stand on, although judging by the thick layer of moss that covered it, nobody had stood on it for ages. I swam over and hoisted myself up.

The mouldy brick walls of the chamber slanted upwards. From eight or nine storeys above me, a little light trickled down from the cavern's roof, through what looked like a grating. Was it big enough for me to squeeze through, assuming I could get up there and open it? I didn't know, but I couldn't see any other option.

Rising up along the wall was another series of jutting bricks. I put my foot cautiously on the lowest one … and it crumbled away to nothing. I tried again. It crumbled. I grabbed for a brick at hand level, and it crumbled, too.

Darn it. Darn it. Darn it. I was stuck down here. Lady Roslyn obviously wasn't coming after me, because if she had dived in after me, she would already have come shooting in. She must be lost somewhere else in the sewers – and since she had the umbrella, that meant the glowing drop was lost, too. Nobody else knew where I was. And nobody else, I realized, knew where my mom was. I was going to die down here, and Mom was going to rot away in whatever awful monster prison they had thrown her into.

I dropped to my knees and took in a big choking breath, ready to burst into tears ... and then I stopped.

Because there was something funny about that breath. It tasted just a teeny bit less foul. And come to think of it, if I concentrated, I could feel just a little bit of a breeze on my wet face. But where was it coming from?

There! Right behind the first brick I had crumbled – there was a little hole. I scraped away with my fingernails and it got big enough for me to stick two fingers in, so I stuck two fingers in and pulled with them both until it got big enough to stick my whole hand in, and then I pulled until I could fit two hands in, and I kept going until it was big enough for me to fit in.

Before I crawled in, I paused for just a moment.

The opening I had made was pitch black. I had no idea where it led. All I knew was that there was a steady breeze of fresh air coming out of it. Was that enough?

Heck, yes, it was. I crawled in. And I kept crawling.

It wasn't easy. The rough bricks scraped my knees through the tattered remains of my jeans, and if I lifted my head too much, I'd scrape that, too. But the breeze on my face kept me going. Then the tunnel started tilting upwards. And then I saw a dim light up ahead, and that kept me going even faster.

Finally, I reached the end, and I climbed out.

I was in a pit, and the third-best thing of all was, it was completely dry.

The *second*-best thing was that there was a grating in the ceiling above me, and it was at most two storeys above. It was close enough to smell fresh air and hear traffic.

And the best thing of all was, there were iron rungs in the wall. Sturdy-looking, rust-free iron rungs that led upwards, straight to the grate.

I started climbing. I got about halfway and my arm muscles just quit. I couldn't blame them, I guess – I had asked them to do an awful lot. "I'm giving you a minute, arms," I told them. "After that, I expect action."

My arms chittered back at me, which was not something they had ever done before. Then I heard the chittering noise again and realized it wasn't coming from my arms. It was coming from a pipe on the wall, level with my head. There was a scraggly rat standing just inside it. I started.

"Don't mind me," I told him. "I'm just leaving."

The rat chittered again, very loudly. And then I realized I wasn't hearing a rat. I was hearing *rats*. Lots of rats. *Maybe I'd better move out of the way*, I thought, but I was about three seconds too late. Thousands of rats exploded out of the pipe, crashing into my face, knocking me back down to the ground, swarming over me.

During the creepiest and most disgusting day of my entire life, I thought I had handled everything pretty calmly, all things considered. But now there were rats swarming over my body, and all I could do was shriek really intelligent things like *"Aaaaaaa!"* or "GET OFF GET OFF GETOFFGETOFFOFFOFFOFF!"

The rats didn't listen.

And just when I thought there was nothing grosser than rats swarming over me, they started swarming *under* me, too. I could feel myself starting to float away on a tide of rats. I stopped thrashing and grabbed for the nearest metal rung, but it was a little too high, and before I could sit upright, I was swept away by the rodent tide, into another dark tunnel.

"No!" I yelled, as the sunlight and fresh air vanished. "NO NO NO NO!!" But the tunnel they were sweeping down was so narrow that I couldn't spread my arms, couldn't sit up, couldn't roll over. I couldn't do anything but be swept along by a current that was even grosser than the sewage that had swept me along before.

Suddenly, the rats and I plummeted off a ledge into a wider hallway, and my back clanged up against a grating. Its bars were close enough together to stop me, but not the rats, and they kept swarming over and around me on their way through. Inside my head, two thoughts were chasing each other in a frantic circle, and finally, *Get up and run!* won out over *Keep screaming until you pass out.*

But with an avalanche of rats weighing me down, I couldn't even sit up. All I could do was lift up my head, which let me see a carpet of rats stretching off all the way to a bend in the hallway, a dozen feet away. Maybe I should have kept my head down.

One particularly brave rat leapt onto my face. I growled at it and snapped my teeth. It jumped back as far as my shoulder, but it didn't go any farther. It just stood there, looking back at me with a defiant expression.

I guess it called my bluff. No way was I going to actually bite it, and it knew it, and I knew it knew it, and—

There was something coming around the corner. It was a moving lump of rats.

No. Not a lump of rats: a lump *under* the rats. Something the size of a small horse was barrelling towards me, sending the rats spraying up in front of it.

The rat on my shoulder must have seen it, too, because its eyes opened wide in panic. It leapt off me just as the lump arrived and started shaking itself furiously, sending rats flying like a wet dog shaking drops of water into the air.

Except this wasn't a dog. It was a pig.

A pig wearing a bathing suit.

A *huge* pig wearing a bathing suit.

A bathing-suit-wearing pig so big, it could make eye contact with a cow.

CHAPTER 10

*R*ight now, there weren't any cows handy, so the pig got busy flattening rats. And biting rats. And squashing rats against the wall with its thick, bristly back.

The sight was simultaneously beautiful and terrifying: beautiful because the pig was doing exactly what I wished I could have done to the rats; terrifying because he might do it to *me* next.

The rats, obviously, came down squarely on the side of terrified. Squealing in panic, the tide of rodents flowed out as quickly as it had flowed in – all except for one rat, which sprinted back towards me. I recognized its defiant expression. It leaned over the tattered remains of my jeans and bit my ankle.

"OWWW!" I yelled. I stomped my foot and waved

my leg, trying to shake off the slimy little jerk, but it hung on with its disgusting tiny paws.

The giant pig spotted the rat and roared in anger. (Yes, he *roared*. No, I didn't think a pig could roar, either. Trust me, at that moment, it was a beautiful sound.) The pig swooped down, teeth bared, then grabbed the rat's ear and yanked it off me. The pig shook the rat furiously until it went flying, crashed into the wall, and tumbled back to the ground with a splash.

The rat turned and brandished its tiny fist in anger. Then it clapped its paw against the bloody spot on its head where its ear had been and ran squealing off.

The pig turned towards me.

I sat there as still as I could. I didn't know what you had to do to enrage a pig, but I figured complete inaction was the least likely alternative.

The pig – or, wait, was it a boar? I never knew the difference – either way, he lowered his head. To charge? I broke my ban on motion enough to shrink back as far as I could.

But he didn't charge. He lowered his snout into a box that was tied to his neck and began rifling around in it. Finally, he grabbed something out of it with his teeth and gave it to me.

It was a business card. A fancy business card, printed with expensive-looking embossed lettering. In the middle was an odd name. And below that, where the profession would normally go, was a single word:

I relaxed a little. I was pretty sure wild animals didn't hand out business cards before charging. "I'm Hyacinth," I told him.

I was trying to figure out whether pigs shook hands when he bowed to me. Something about him was so courtly and dignified that I curtsied back. (Or, I guess, I mimed a curtsy, since an actual curtsy would have required standing in a skirt, instead of sitting down in a shredded pair of sewage-covered blue jeans.)

Then the pig rooted around in the cards and handed me two more.

"Not at all. You got here just in time."
Oaroboarus handed me another card.

I WOULD BE MOST OBLIGED
IF YOU WOULD FOLLOW ME.

"Sure. Why not?" I said. I knew from my grand-mother's farm how pigs lived, and if he took me home to a damp pile of oozy mud – well, under the circumstances, that would be like moving into the Ritz.

Oaroboarus led me down the passage to an inter-section, where a huge current flowed by. Somehow, I knew it was the Tyburn again. Downstream, I could see a warm, inviting light coming from a brick door-way. It looked like a short trip to get there, but when Oaroboarus saw me looking at it, he shook his massive head and led me in the opposite direction.

Then he led me through a series of twists and turns, and we ended up at the exact same doorway I had just seen.

"Couldn't we have gone the direct route?" I asked.

EASY PATHS
DO NOT INTEREST ME.

"Um, OK," I said.

We passed through the doorway into a round brick chamber lit by a cast-iron stove. Pipes sprouted from the stove, zigzagging across the room to a dozen different clanking, steaming devices. I had no idea what some of them were, but one of them – a contraption of rods and wheels, as tall as a refrigerator and as wide as a car – was an old-fashioned printing press, *thump-thump-thump*ing away.

Standing on a step stool so that he could reach the press was a boy who looked a little bit younger than me. I'd say he was in Year 7 or so, but his clothes were like no Year 7's I'd ever seen. They were so huge for him, and so out-of-date, that it looked like he had raided his grandfather's closet. In the flickering of the stove, I couldn't tell whether his wild hair was dark blond or light brown. His smile was quiet but unmistakable, as if whatever he was printing amused him in a way that only he could understand.

As I stood there, trying to figure him out, the iron stove's warmth seeped into my bones a bit, and I finally realized how cold and damp I had been. I started to shiver, and no matter how hard I tried to control it, I could feel my teeth chattering.

At the sound, the boy looked up from the printing press. "Oaroboarus! You brought me a guest!"

Oaroboarus handed him two cards.

"Gross!" the boy said. "Well, the rats won't come in here. They hate the noise of the printing press. I'm Little Ben."

"I'm Hy-Hy-Hy—" I started to say, but I was shivering and chattering too much to get the words out.

Little Ben looked concerned. He hopped down and carried his stool over to the wall, where there was a tall cabinet stretching all the way up to the ceiling. It had twenty-six narrow drawers, each one labelled with a letter of the alphabet.

"Let's see," he said. "I'm guessing it would be under B."

Leaning against the cabinet was a stick with a pair of grabber claws at the end. Little Ben took it and, standing on his stool, reached upwards with it and pulled out the B drawer. Then he reached in with the grabber and pulled out a blanket, which he handed to me.

It smelled a little musty. I didn't care. I wrapped it around myself gratefully.

He reached into a lower drawer marked T, pulled out a cup with a tea bag already in it, and poured hot water into it from a kettle on the iron stove. Then he pulled a pitcher of milk out of M, poured some in, and handed the cup to me. "Sit there and drink some tea and warm up," he said.

While I tried to stop shivering, Little Ben turned to Oaroboarus. "I printed up those cards you wanted," he said. He took a large sheet of stiff paper out of the press and held it out so Oaroboarus could read it. I caught a glimpse of a few of the phrases on it:

I SHOULD
BE OBLIGED
IF YOU WOULD
EXAMINE MY

EXACTLY SO

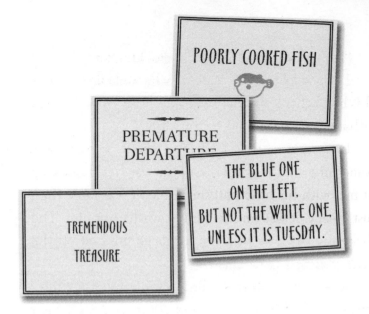

POORLY COOKED FISH

PREMATURE
DEPARTURE

TREMENDOUS
TREASURE

THE BLUE ONE
ON THE LEFT,
BUT NOT THE WHITE ONE,
UNLESS IT IS TUESDAY.

Oaroboarus gave a satisfied nod, and Little Ben pulled his step stool over to another large clanking gadget. He slid the paper into it. After a few seconds of steaming and snipping, the gadget spat the paper back out, now cut into a collection of little cards. Oaroboarus picked them up in his mouth and deposited them in the box around his neck.

By now, I had unfrozen enough to speak. "I'm Hyacinth. Do you live down here?"

"Yup."

"All by yourself?"

"I've got Oaroboarus to look after me." He patted the pig's flank, and Oaroboarus gave a friendly snort. "How about you? Do you live in the sewers, too?"

"I'm just visiting," I said. "I'm looking for—"

I stopped, because I realized: what did I know about this boy, other than that he lived in a sewer with a pig? What reason did I have to trust him?

In fact, now that I thought about it, there was something a little creepy about the way he was looking at me, with his little half-smile. No, it was more than just creepy. It was *sinister*. And it wasn't just him. The flickering shadows that the furnace's fire cast on the brick ceiling ... the smell of sewage wafting through the red-brick archway ... the endless pounding of the steaming machines ... this was not a good place, and nobody who lived here could be a good person.

My skin started to crawl. I threw off the blanket and leapt to my feet.

"Is something wrong?" Little Ben said.

I backed away from him, towards the exit. Oaroboarus leapt forwards and snarled at me, all pretence of courtliness gone. *Move slowly*, I thought. *Don't provoke him. You saw what he did to those rats. He'll do the same to you! He'll tear you apart! RUN!*

I turned around and ran.

And I immediately ran into something. I slammed my fist against it in a blind panic, yelling "AAAAAAAH!"

CHAPTER 11

"I'm delighted to see you, too," Lady Roslyn said. I stopped hitting her and tried to calm down. She put one hand on my shoulder. The other one held the umbrella, which was glowing from within – it looked like she had managed to hang on to the missing drop. She turned to Little Ben. "If you've harmed her in the slightest…"

Little Ben blinked at her with feigned innocence. "Why would I hurt her? I was hoping we could be friends."

Lady Roslyn spotted the teacup lying on the ground, where I had dropped it in my panic. She gasped. "You drank tea with him?"

"He seemed harmless!"

"This is important, Hyacinth. Did he put the milk in first or second?"

I stared at her. I felt like my panic was ebbing away, but I was still not exactly thinking clearly, and I was kind of confused about why we were discussing tea service when we ought to be running away. Running away from what, I couldn't say. I just knew there was something terrifying in that room, and I needed to get away from it fast.

"First or second?"

"He put the tea bag in first, then the water, then the milk."

"Oh, dear God in Heaven," Lady Roslyn said.

"Would you like some tea, too?" Little Ben asked her, with that same smug smile.

Before she could answer, Oaroboarus lunged for her, teeth snapping.

We ran.

To my surprise (and relief), Little Ben didn't even try to follow us as we ran out of the archway and jumped into the Tyburn.

Oaroboarus was a different story.

As we struggled upstream, he swam behind us, his

thick pig legs paddling steadily. He never managed to gain on us, but he didn't seem to be getting tired, and I was already exhausted. On the plus side, I was feeling too worn out to keep panicking.

"How much longer?" I gasped.

"No idea," Lady Roslyn panted. "Quite lost."

At that, I found the energy to panic. What scared me wasn't that we were lost. It was that Lady Roslyn was too tired to whip up an ornately sarcastic reply. That meant we were in trouble.

Plus, Oaroboarus was now catching up to us. We were getting slower and slower, and he was getting closer and closer.

If only that darn pig weren't so stubborn—

That's when I had an inspiration. I knew exactly why Oaroboarus had taken me the long way around to get to Little Ben's lair, instead of just floating downstream. It was because he was too ... well, *pigheaded* to take the easy way out. I mean, nobody ever said "as easygoing as a pig", did they?

And that meant that as long as we were fighting our way upstream, we'd never lose him. But if we just turned around...

"Follow me," I told Lady Roslyn as I spun around and dove past Oaroboarus, who by now was right behind us. He looked at me like I was crazy, and so did

Lady Roslyn. Then she shrugged and dove past him, too.

I swam frantically for a few moments, then looked over my shoulder. Oaroboarus was floating back where we had left him. I never thought pigs had very expressive faces, but I could see by his conflicted look that he was struggling, trying to make himself take the easy path of swimming downstream.

Finally, with a resigned sigh, he reached into his box, pulled out two cards, and cast them onto the water.

They floated down to me.

The threat didn't bother me. In fact, I wasn't feeling afraid at all any more. Maybe my newfound courage was just a caffeine buzz from the tea, but it felt like something more. It felt like I could figure anything out.

I floated along for a few minutes, letting the current

carry me. With the umbrella closed tightly around the glowing drop of water, we couldn't use it to cast a magic circle of light, so the sewage was just sewage. But if I closed my eyes and remembered the clean, clear river hard enough, it almost felt like I was back in it.

"Where will the current take us?" I asked Lady Roslyn.

"I don't know this stretch of the Tyburn well," Lady Roslyn said, "but it eventually leads into the Thames. First, though, we'll go right past Little Ben's lair. But of course you considered that before you arbitrarily changed our direction."

"Nothing to worry about," I said, because as soon as I thought about it, I suddenly knew what would happen. "He didn't bother chasing us in the first place. I get the feeling he won't even bother sticking his head out as we pass."

"You seem to think you know an awful lot about that creature," Lady Roslyn said. "Well, I know much more than you do. And I know that ... that *thing* doesn't always take the form of a young boy."

I could feel my confidence ebbing as mysteriously as it had arrived. "What other forms have you seen?"

"I think, my dear, that this is another question it would be better not to answer."

By now, I knew not to push her – and, besides,

maybe she was right. Maybe I *didn't* want to know what that thing really looked like. "When you showed up, you asked if he had put the milk in first—"

"That's right. The British didn't always drink tea, you know. Haven't you ever wondered how boiled leaves from a Chinese bush became our national drink?"

I could see where she was going. "You put it in hot water—"

"That's right. And when you do, it binds with some of the water's magic and makes it less potent. In fact, if you put milk in first, it neutralizes the magic completely. But if you put the milk in second, you reverse everything, and the magic is more powerful than it ever was."

"But why would Little Ben want to give me a magical drink?"

"It's entirely possible that he was giving you some wonderful, generous magical gift. But *some* people – less charitably inclined than I – might guess he was casting a spell on you. It seemed to me that you had some sort of ... let's say 'inspiration' about how Oaroboarus would behave, didn't you?"

"Yeah, but—"

"Followed immediately by an inspiration about what Little Ben would or would not do? I'm sure your lucky guesses have absolutely *nothing* to do with any sort of magical link that might have been created. He couldn't possibly be spying on us through your eyes at this very moment."

We floated past the entrance to Little Ben's lair. As we did, I got a glimpse of him through the archway. He was back on his step stool, bent over his printing press, with his back to us. He didn't even look up as we passed. I had been right about that, but now I wasn't sure it was much of a cause for celebration.

We both kept quiet until we had floated out of his earshot. Finally, I said, "So why *isn't* he chasing us?"

"The kindly old woman with whom you are enjoying a gentle float is sure it's just because he's a tolerant, live-and-let-live sort of chap. Somebody more cynical might ask: does he really need to follow you, if he can already see through your eyes?"

We floated along for a little while, until Lady Roslyn finally broke the silence. "If you get any more inspirations," she said, "it might do to mention them to me at once."

CHAPTER 12

The river sped up. It turned into a waterfall and spurted us over the edge.

With a splash and a clang, we landed in a puddle of water, just deep enough to break our fall. I staggered to my feet and looked around. We were surrounded by four iron walls that must have been fifteen feet high. Three of them were hidden behind thick waterfalls. The fourth was a mass of solid iron. The floor we had landed on was a big grating, dotted with thousands of holes, so that the water never got higher than a small pool.

"How do we get out?" I asked.

"Oh, am I in charge again? How kind of you, but really, I wouldn't dream of imposing my will."

Well, fine. I wasn't going to apologize again. I was the one who had gotten us away from a giant angry pig and an evil tea-using magician. If she wanted me to be in charge, I'd be in charge.

I strode confidently over to the one wall that wasn't blocked by a waterfall and climbed up it.

Or, at least, I tried. It was wet and smooth, and I didn't accomplish much more than breaking a nail.

I tried again. This time, I accomplished twice as much. I broke two nails.

"Fine!" I said to Lady Roslyn, who was not trying very hard to hide her amusement. "What would you do?"

"I? I would have kept going upstream, and we would have reached the surface very quickly—"

"We didn't look very quick to me."

She ignored me. "At present, the best option seems to be waiting here while you attempt to claw handholds into solid iron."

I found the whole thing much less funny than Lady Roslyn seemed to. Maybe that was because it wasn't *her* mother who was being held hostage by monsters in who-knew-what kind of horrible dungeon.

I wished my family were there. Time and time again, when Mom had gotten us into some horrible fix, my grandmother or one of my aunts had bailed us out. But they weren't there now, and I was on my own.

Or was I? What was it my grandmother's note had said, before it disappeared? *Your aunts and I have done what we can to prepare you. As long as you remember, I will always be with you.*

Well, I was pretty sure nobody had prepared me for being in a wet, smelly iron prison …

… Wait a minute. Maybe somebody had.

I always loved it when Aunt Talia babysat, because she'd let me stay up late while she told me endless bedtime stories. And one of my favourites had been about a princess trapped in a pit in the centre of a wet, smelly maze. A maze whose walls were made out of iron! I always thought it was just a story – but was she preparing me for this? Did my aunts somehow know what was going to happen? As soon as I got a working phone, I was going to call them and demand some answers.

But in the meantime, I tried to remember how the princess in the story had escaped. None of the princes could find her, so she had to take matters into her own hands. She put her ears up to the iron wall, and she could hear the footsteps of the nearest prince. Then she banged a message to him, telling him the secret of the maze so he could get a ladder to her.

It was worth a try. I pressed my ear to the wall and

concentrated. At first, all I could hear was a rumbling sound, which I knew came from the water pouring into the room. But as I listened, I gradually made out another, more rhythmic sound. Footsteps? Maybe.

I banged on the wall, then listened again. All was quiet. If the noise I had heard before was footsteps, then maybe whoever was making them had stopped to listen.

Aunt Talia never specified how exactly the princess managed to tell the prince anything more useful than "BANG BANG BANG". But on another occasion, my aunt Topsy had taught me Morse code. Of course, a code was only useful if the person on the other end knew it, too. Still, there was one Morse code phrase that more people knew than any other, and it happened to apply here.

I hammered out three fast bangs, then three slow, then three fast: "SOS."

I waited, holding my breath. Silence for a moment. And then, through the wall, from far away, the footsteps again. No – they weren't footsteps. Somebody was stomping. Stomping in Morse code, one letter at a time.

"W-H-E-R-E A-R-E Y-O-U?"

I banged back, "S-Q-U-A-R-E R-O-O-M. 3 W-A-L-L-S W-A-T-E-R-F-A-L-L-S. 1 W-A-L-L D-R-Y."

Again, a moment of silence. And then: "H-A-N-G

O-N. T-H-E-R-E I-N 5 M-I-N-U-T-E-S."

Those five minutes gave me time to wonder. Unless there was some underground society of telegraph operators, the odds must have been pretty small that anybody in earshot knew Morse code. Had I just gotten lucky? Or was this more evidence that my aunts somehow knew all this would happen?

I hadn't reached any conclusion when I heard footsteps coming from the dry corridor above our heads. A few moments later, somebody stuck his head over the wall.

I thought he was about my age, but I couldn't be sure, because his face was hidden by shadows. Then he cocked his head, and the shadows didn't shift from their places on his face. Those black smudges weren't actually shadows, then. I didn't want to think about what they actually were.

"Oozidge, den?" he said.

"Um, I'm sorry?" I said.

I guess he thought that was a funny response to whatever question he had asked, because he grinned. It was such a charming grin that I found myself smiling back, even though I kind of had the feeling he was laughing at me.

"Wujdee madder, you doh speak inlidge??" he asked.

"Um," I said again.

"This gentleman," Lady Roslyn said, "initially inquired as to our identity. His subsequent question expressed doubt that you understood the English language. You must excuse her, sir." Lady Roslyn dropped her voice as if she were about to tell him some kind of horrible secret. "She's from *America*."

He tapped a smudged hand on his smudged forehead. "Shay no mower," he said, and I guessed he meant "Say no more." I felt like my ears were getting used to his accent, kind of like my eyes had gotten used to the dark down here. So when he added, "Si tie. Oil be rye ba," I was pretty sure he meant "Sit tight. I'll be right back."

He vanished, and his footsteps faded away.

"Who was that, and why did he talk like that?"

"He is a tosher," Lady Roslyn said. "A scavenger. Powerful artifacts collect down here, and ordinary objects gain power once they're down here long enough. You can eke out a living looking among the rubbish for tosh, as they call it. Provided, of course, you don't mind dressing like a tramp and stinking like something worse. The toshers have been living down here for centuries, passing their dialect (and their unwashed clothes) from generation to generation."

A few moments later, the footsteps *click-clack*ed back, and the young man peered over the edge again.

He made a series of strange noises that, I realized, meant "I forgot to introduce myself. I'm Newfangled Troy."

Somebody else peered over the edge, with the longest face I had ever seen. He looked a few years older than Troy. "I'm Longface Lucky," he said with the same accent.

A third face peered over the edge. It was as round as Longface's was long. When this person spoke, he had the same accent as the other two. Like Longface Lucky, I would say he was in his late teens. "I'm Richard the Raker," he said.

I wondered if everybody who lived underground had a weird nickname. I had always thought my name was kind of bizarre, but now it was feeling almost plain. "I'm just Hyacinth," I said.

"Better to be 'just' than 'longface' or 'newfangled', ain't it?" said Troy, with a wink. "Well, gents, shall we get them out of there?"

"Just one minute," said Longface Lucky. "Newfangled Troy, what with him being newfangled and all, he don't know who he's got down in this hole. But I ain't so newfangled, and I know Lady Roslyn when I sees her."

"Well, what of it?" Lady Roslyn asked.

"Well, the what of it is, I don't know if a hole ain't

such a bad place to keep Lady Roslyn when you got the chance to keep her in one."

"Lady Roslyn and the toshers ain't exactly on Friend Street, if you see what I mean," Richard the Raker added.

"What about the girl?" asked Newfangled Troy. "I don't hear as you're saying she done nothing. It don't seem what you'd call chivalrous to leave her down there."

Lucky's long face didn't look impressed. "If she's one of Lady Roslyn's gang, it don't seem what you'd call smart to take her with us, neither."

"We ain't done so well with Lady Roslyn's chadwicks, neither, if you see what I mean," Richard the Raker added.

"So that's settled, then," Lucky said. "You're staying down in the hole, and we bid you good day. But don't you ladies worry. It ain't forecast to rain up above for another hour yet, which therefore this chamber ain't going to start filling up too fast for the drain to empty for another ninety minutes, which therefore you ain't going to drown for ninety-two minutes roughly, depending as how long you can holds your breath." He tapped his forehead politely. All three of them pulled their heads out of sight.

CHAPTER 13

"We can pay you," I said. Immediately, the heads reappeared.

"Well now, why didn't you say so up front?" Long-face said.

"If you've got the millbank, we ain't so thorny, if you see what I mean," Richard the Raker added.

"Come to think of it, what you got in that there glowing umbrella might recompense us for our troubles," said Longface.

"What I have in the umbrella," Lady Roslyn said, "would cause you far more trouble than you imagine."

"Well, now, that may be so, and that may be not."

"You know full well I can't lie to you here."

Longface Lucky and Richard the Raker looked at

each other and laughed. "There's an awful lot of tosh-ers what would find that awful funny," Lucky said, "if only they wasn't so dead."

"I promised Short-Nose Jack I would tell him how to find the source of the Tyburn, and I kept that prom-ise. I didn't promise to hold his hand for the entire expedition. If I had, *I* wouldn't have let his men die."

"We ain't saying you'd be such a lollard as to lie outright," Richard the Raker said. "But when it comes to phrasing things, you may be going round the glass-house, if you see what I mean."

"Very well," Lady Roslyn said, holding up the umbrella. "See for yourself."

Longface Lucky nodded to Newfangled Troy, and Newfangled Troy lowered what looked like a hoe over the wall. The handle must have been eight or nine feet long. By stretching out his arms, Troy was able to lower it far enough for Lady Roslyn to hook the umbrella over it.

Newfangled Troy started to raise it up, but before it was halfway there, Longface stopped him. "Hold on just a minute." He stuck his head down, peering into the umbrella from a few feet away, then let out a low whistle. "Well, boil me in Betty," he said. "You wasn't half joking. Put that back down, Newfangled Troy. You oughtn't be touching that with an eight-foot pole."

I had no idea what he was talking about, but I

knew one thing: I was going to have to start saying "boil me in Betty".

Troy lowered the hoe, and Lady Roslyn took the umbrella back.

"Would you take Lady Roslyn's ribbon?" I said. "It was tied around the umbrella when it went through the Lost Property Office, so maybe it absorbed some magic. That would make it tosh, wouldn't it?"

"We'll sees about that," Longface said. "Let's have a sniff."

Lady Roslyn hesitated for a moment, as if she wasn't willing to give the ribbon up. Then, reluctantly, she took it out of her hair and tied it around the hoe.

This time, Longface Lucky let Troy lift the hoe all the way up. He took the ribbon, held it up to his sharply pointed nose, and inhaled, swishing the scent around his nostrils like I had seen my dad do with wine in his cheeks. "Very nice. Circle line, ain't it? Fresh, too. And is that – no. Can't be. Can it?" He looked at us in amazement.

I wondered what he smelled. Actually, I wondered why he wanted to smell *anything*. If I could have, I would have been holding my breath the entire time we had been down in the sewers. But whatever he smelled, it was impressive. He nodded at us.

"Good enough?" I asked.

"Good enough, and three kinds of better. You have the word of a tosher: we'll get you out of that hole and show you the way to the surface, if that's whereas you want to go."

Troy lowered the hoe back down. Lady Roslyn grabbed on to it, and Troy and Richard pulled her up. Then they lowered it and pulled me up, too.

Now that I was standing next to them and not just looking at them from below, I could see their bodies as well as their faces, and they didn't quite match up like I would have expected. Longface Lucky's long face was on a hugely round body. He looked like a snowman with a baguette for a head.

On the other hand, Richard the Raker's round face was on a long and scrawny body. He looked like a scarecrow with a watermelon on top.

Newfangled Troy, though... He was just right. He had not only a cute face but a really cute stomach, which I hadn't even thought was a thing, but it was. I could see it because he and his friends were shirtless. All they had on were canvas trousers and long velveteen coats with lots of bulging pockets. Each of them had one of those long hoes in one hand and a lantern in the other. Also, Troy had a cute stomach. Did I mention that? I probably mentioned that. It was definitely a thing.

Say something intelligent, Hyacinth, I thought. I opened my mouth, but nothing came out, intelligent or otherwise. Newfangled Troy didn't seem to mind. He winked at me. His face was dirty enough that I couldn't see much other than his eyes, but up close, they were really nice eyes.

I hoped my own face was dirty enough to hide how much I was blushing.

Longface Lucky started walking. His two friends followed him, with Lady Roslyn and me behind.

I whispered to Lady Roslyn, "What he said about his friends who died—"

"I believe I have already offered a satisfactory explanation," she said, and I had a feeling that was all I was going to get out of her.

The toshers led us through a maze of passages, turning at every intersection we came to. A couple of times, I recognized places we had already been, which made me pretty sure they were just trying to confuse us. Maybe they didn't want us to be able to find wherever they were taking us on our own.

Finally, the tunnel ended in a sight I never expected to see down in the sewers: two beautifully carved wooden doors, set in a stone arch covered with gargoyles.

Longface Lucky turned to Lady Roslyn. "Now,

anything what we finds in here belongs to us, don't it?"

"I rather doubt that anything you'd find would interest us," Lady Roslyn said, but Longface simply stood there, waiting, until she sighed and added, "Fine. Anything *what you finds* belongs to you."

Longface nodded to Richard the Raker, who pulled a small set of wire tools out of one pocket. He stuck them into the iron lock and wriggled them around, and in a few moments, there was a *click*. The doors swung open.

The toshers stepped in, and I followed them.

As far as I could tell, we weren't in the sewers any more. We were in a massive, non-smelly cathedral, with row after row of empty pews, and stone ceilings arching way overhead.

Or maybe it wasn't an actual cathedral, because I couldn't see any religious symbols. And the beautiful stained-glass windows showed stories that weren't from any Bible I had ever read. Most of them were totally mysterious to me, like one showing a big stone covered with Egyptian symbols sinking underwater.

But I did recognize others, like the one showing men in top hats holding handkerchiefs over their noses as they ran out of a fancy-looking building. And not just any building: it was Parliament. *The Great Stink!* I thought.

The window next to it showed a sink with separate hot and cold water taps. It looked a lot like the sink in Aunt Polly's flat. No, wait – those were the exact same black-and-white tiles on the wall behind the sink. It didn't just look like Aunt Polly's flat – it *was* Aunt Polly's flat. Was there some connection between this building and my family?

I looked around for more clues, but nothing else seemed to have much to do with me. Weirdly, the highest set of stained-glass windows was entirely blank. They were just big tinted rectangles, glowing as if the sun were setting behind them.

In fact, the higher I looked, the less finished the building seemed. On the floor under my feet, the tiles were crazy detailed. I had to kneel down to make out the millions of tiny figures, all doing everyday stuff like cooking or sewing. Just above that, at ankle level, the wall was nearly as busy with stone and wood carvings. But as you went higher and higher on the wall, there were fewer and fewer carvings, until you got to a row of carved stone scrolls with no words on them. And above them, there were just blank walls and those blank stained-glass windows, under a plain stone roof.

"Here's what I don't savoy," said Richard the Raker. "Every time we comes here, there ain't nobody else here. Every time we leaves here, we leaves the door open. And every time as we come back, that door there is locked again. So who's doing all that locking, if you know what I mean?"

Longface Lucky shrugged. He didn't look especially interested in big questions. Instead, he started shining his lantern all around, looking for something. The other two toshers followed him, searching in the carved nooks as they went.

"Where are we?" I whispered to Lady Roslyn.

"Every one of the secret rivers has a sacred place – a sort of a basin in which some portion of its power collects. This would appear to be the sacred place of the Tyburn."

That made sense, kind of. Maybe all the little people on the floor tiles were the people who had lived along the Tyburn over thousands of years. Maybe the stained-glass windows showed things that had happened at some point in the river's history. And if the magical drop of water I had unleashed into the river was as powerful as Lady Roslyn said – well, maybe Aunt Polly's sink was now part of the river's history, too.

One thing still puzzled me. "The biggest windows are still blank and so are all those scrolls. If this is such an important place, why isn't it finished?"

"Nothing's ever finished," Lady Roslyn said.

That was her least useful answer yet, which was

saying a lot. But I didn't have the chance to ask her more, because Richard the Raker yelled, "Aha!"

He shined his lantern behind the base of a massive stone arch while the other toshers crowded around. "Found some tosh?" asked Longface Lucky.

"Send me off to Sackville, this ain't no tosh," said Richard the Raker. "This here is what you'd call a tosheroon. In fact, this may just be *the* tosheroon, if you know what I mean." He knelt down and picked up a funny-looking object, and I recognized it immediately.

It was the wrench-hammer-hacksaw tool I'd used to fix my tap.

I guess I should have thought before I said what I said next. I should have noticed that Richard the Raker and Newfangled Troy and Longface Lucky were all gazing at the tool in silent awe. I should have remembered that they didn't trust me to begin with. I should have kept my mouth shut.

But I was so surprised to see the thing that had started the whole adventure that I couldn't help myself. "That's mine!" I exclaimed.

The toshers' awed expressions vanished. Instead, Newfangled Troy looked puzzled. Richard the Raker looked suspicious.

And Longface Lucky? He looked really, really, *really* suspicious.

"Now, now, Hyacinth," said Lady Roslyn. "We've agreed: what these gentlemen find, they may keep."

"She didn't say as she wants to take it," Longface Lucky said. "She said as it was hers already."

"How could that possibly be hers?" Lady Roslyn said.

"I notice you ain't saying it ain't," Longface Lucky said.

"I think I made myself perfectly clear," Lady Roslyn said.

Longface Lucky took the wrench-hammer-hacksaw from Richard the Raker and gave it a deep sniff with that sharp nose of his. His eyes narrowed. "See, what's interesting about this situation here is, we finds you awandering with an umbrella full of something remarkable, and a young woman at your side, and a ribbon what smells of some things which is quite unusual in their own rights. And all along, I was wondering how those facts there might be related to each other. And now here's the young woman, saying as she owns Bazalgette's Trowel. And now here's you, going around the glasshouse on the question of whether it is hers or it ain't."

"If you're implying that I'm deliberately misleading you, then you are a very sceptical man," Lady Roslyn said, which only made Longface look even more sceptical. I couldn't blame him. I mean, *I* could tell she was dodging the question, and I didn't even know what they were talking about.

"You know what I think, gents," Longface said. "I think as we've found ourselves *two* tosheroons today. One of them is Bazalgette's Trowel, which would be snowy enough ... and the other is this young lady here."

Longface held out his long hoe, blocking us in on one side. Richard the Raker did the same, trapping us on the other.

Keeping her eyes on them, Lady Roslyn took a few steps backwards. Since there wasn't anywhere else to go, I did the same thing. We bumped into the wooden entrance doors, which had somehow closed behind us.

I spun around and yanked on the handle.

The doors were locked. We were trapped.

CHAPTER 14

"*Y*ou gave us your word," Lady Roslyn said.

"I promised you as we'd get you out of that hole, what we did. And I promised as we'd show you the way to the surface. Well, see those stone steps there?" Longface Lucky pointed to an archway a football field away from us. "That's the way up. Now I've shown it to you. I never promised as I'd let you actually take it. You ain't the only one what knows your way around a glasshouse, Lady Roslyn. Now, gents, let's finish this off—"

"It's not my thingy," I said.

"Hyacinth…" Lady Roslyn said.

Her tone of voice made it clear she wanted me to stop, but I didn't see how bluffing could make the situation any worse, so I kept going. "That thingy there – Battleship's Trowel? I've never seen it before."

"HYACINTH!" Lady Roslyn yelled. She looked genuinely upset.

Great, I thought. *Way to spoil my bluff.* But I didn't let her distract me. I kept going. "Anyway, it's true. I've never seen that tool thing. I just said it's mine because it looked pretty, so I don't have any connection to it, which means I can't be a tosheroon thingy, whatever that is, so you can go ahead and lift the hoe thingy, and you can keep the trowel thingy, and we'll be on our way." (Fun fact about me: when I'm lying, my thingy-per-minute count goes through the roof.)

I stopped and took a deep breath. I was waiting to see if the toshers would believe me. Weirdly, they seemed to be waiting for something, too. And so did Lady Roslyn. They all looked up nervously, and then down nervously, and then around nervously. And when nothing happened, they all looked at each other in relief.

"Well," said Longface Lucky. "I suppose as you must be telling the truth, seeing as how the sky ain't fallen."

Unfortunately, at exactly that moment, the sky *did* fall.

Well, not the sky. If the actual sky had fallen, that wouldn't have been so bad, since presumably it's made of nice soft clouds and the occasional bird.

But what actually started falling was the ceiling. Which was made of gigantic blocks of stone.

One of which crashed right next to me, almost smooshing me. Another one smashed into Richard's hoe, shattering it into splinters. A dozen other giant stone blocks pounded the pews around me into sawdust.

"Aha! You *was* lying!" Richard the Raker cried triumphantly, but he wasn't triumphant for very long, because a giant beam of wood came swinging downwards, whamming into him and sending him flying.

Now, usually, I wouldn't be thrilled to have a giant underground cathedral collapsing around my ears. But under those particular circumstances, I could see the bright side, because with Longface's hoe smashed and Richard the Raker whammed, we suddenly had a clear shot at making it to the staircase leading up to the surface.

If we could run to it before the whole building collapsed.

So we ran.

On either side of us, huge stone columns wobbled ominously, threatening to tip onto us as we ran past. Bricks from the walls rained down around us.

Longface Lucky and Newfangled Troy were close

on our heels. We kept running. We were halfway to the steps.

All around the collapsing wall above us, there were alcoves with stone statues, and the statues came tumbling down towards us. A huge stone woman playing a flute toppled into the aisle just in front of me, but with the toshers right behind, I couldn't stop, so I dodged to one side, leapt like a ballerina over a wooden pew, and kept going.

We were three quarters of the way to the steps. Newfangled Troy was barely more than an arm's length behind me, and Longface Lucky was right behind him.

Not too far ahead, I could see the stone steps, curving up out of sight behind an archway. Suddenly, the bottom step snapped up and down. It was like a hand cracking a whip, sending a wave through the tile floor coming right at us.

Since we were in front, Lady Roslyn and I could see that the tile floor was acting like a stormy ocean, and we jumped over the big tile wave. Troy and Longface didn't see it. When the wave reached their feet, they went flying.

We made it to the stairs and started to run up, but the stairs shook and leapt like they were trying to throw us off. We grabbed on to the wooden handrail and pulled ourselves up like mountain climbers.

"What's going on?" I said. Or, actually, shouted, since it was kind of hard to be heard over all the crashing stone.

"When you are in the presence of magic," Lady Roslyn shouted back, "never break your word, and never, never, *never* tell a lie."

We made it to the top of the staircase and staggered out onto a narrow walkway. It led under one of the large blank windows, and now that we were close to it, I could see little silvery fish swimming by outside. This strange cathedral wasn't just underground – it was underwater. And the water was sparkling, like the whole cathedral radiated whatever magic shadow the umbrella did. Maybe that's why I was seeing a beautiful fish-filled river out the window, instead of a brown flow of sewage.

The walkway wasn't wide enough for us to run side by side, and Lady Roslyn, unlike me, didn't stop to gawk at the fish outside the window. She ran on ahead.

I snapped out of it and ran after her.

That's when I noticed that the rumbling and the shaking and the ceiling-collapsing had suddenly stopped. I wondered whether that was a good sign or a bad sign.

I didn't have long to wonder. Just as I passed under the first blank window, the entire walkway jumped with an ear-splitting *BANG*.

One by one, the stones of the walkway began to drop away, crashing to the floor below.

I kept running.

Behind me, I could hear the stones I had just run across crashing down.

I kept running.

The walkway led to an arch, and just as Lady Roslyn ran through it and out of sight, the half dozen feet of walkway between me and her exploded into powder, leaving a huge gap.

I kept running.

I was going to have to jump.

I was going to have to jump right at the very moment I reached the gap, because it was so wide, I wouldn't make it if I jumped a single instant too soon.

I was going to have to jump in half a second.

I was going to have to jump *right now*.

But as my foot hit the last remaining tidbit of walkway, the stone shattered beneath my heel like thin ice.

I couldn't stop. I toppled forwards.

I must have been moving really fast, but everything seemed to go incredibly slowly. I felt like I had all the time in the world to look down and admire the sharp and hard and pointy chunks of stone that were going to be the last things I'd ever see.

Then somebody grabbed the back of my shirt.

I hung there for a moment, and that seemed endless, too. I wanted to know who had me, but after the scraping my clothes had received in the sewers, they were just barely holding together. I could feel my shirt straining, and I knew that if I turned around, the motion would rip it off, and not only would I fall onto a bunch of sharp stones and die, I'd do it topless, which would just make the whole thing embarrassing.

Whoever was holding on to my shirt pulled me back onto the walkway. My feet touched solid ground. I turned around slowly and carefully, and I found myself standing face to face with Newfangled Troy.

There wasn't a whole lot left of this section of stone balcony, which meant there wasn't much room for the two of us, which meant we were standing close together.

I wondered if I should shove him backwards. Sure, he had just saved me, but who knew what he was saving me for? I still didn't know what a tosheroon was, and I certainly didn't know what toshers did to a girl they thought was one. Plus, if I didn't catch up with Lady Roslyn and help her get the drop of water to the Saltpetre Men, I wouldn't see my mom again.

But I couldn't bring myself to do it. Shoving another person to his doom? Sorry, that just wasn't me.

Plus, he smelled really good. It wasn't like anything

you'd expect from somebody who lived in the sewer. It was rugged and clean, like a backyard in winter when someone nearby has a fire going. I'm not saying I would have pushed him to his doom if he had smelled bad. I'm just saying the way he smelled made it a little harder for me to think clearly, and I didn't have very long to think at all, because he grabbed my arms and held them tight at my sides.

"Let me go!" I said.

"You was thinking about pushing me over," he said.

I started to deny it, and then I remembered what had happened the last time I'd lied, so I just settled for glaring at him.

"Ah, I can sees you've had it explained to you about the value of telling the truth. So you know I ain't pulling the wool cap over your eyes whenas I tells you: I'm going to help you." He let go of me.

"Fine," I said. "But *why* are you helping me all of a sudden?"

I was kind of hoping his answer would involve the fact that I smelled as good to him as he smelled to me, although rationally I recognized I wasn't exactly at peak fragrance level. But what he actually said was "A-cause there's money in it for me. See, a tosheroon what belongs to a fellow is a million times more valuable than one what he stole. Magic is a little more cooperative if it thinks as you've got a right to use it. And right now, Bazalgette's Trowel would seem to belong to you. So if you was so kind as to give it to me, I'd be disposed to help you get away."

"You're asking me to give you something that you and your friends already took? Interesting negotiating technique."

"Longface Lucky is a-holding on to it, but it ain't *his*, if you sees what I mean. All you got to do is, tell me as it now belongs to me. Then it's my lookout how I get my hands upon it."

I wasn't sure I wanted to do that. OK, it's not like I even wanted the Trowel, but if it was so incredibly valuable, was it a mistake to give it up?

Then the whole building rumbled again, and the stone balcony under my feet trembled. "Done," I said. "I hereby grant you Bazalgette's Trowel. Much good may it do you. What now?"

"Now? I suppose we stands here and we fights them other two, then whenas that's done, we finds you a way to get out of here."

Over Troy's shoulder, I saw Richard the Raker and Longface Lucky emerge from the steps. Bits of walkway were still sticking out of the wall, like the remaining teeth in a hockey player's mouth, and the two toshers jumped over a few close-together bits until there was just one large gap separating us from them.

"Why ain't you a-grabbed her?" Longface Lucky called over to Newfangled Troy.

"Sorry, friends. I ain't just on her side of this gap. I'm on her side, what you'd call in general."

"WHAT?" roared Longface. "Richard, jump across and wallop 'em both."

"Me, jump?" Richard roared back. "Great maze pond! You jump, if as you're so keen on jumping."

They kept yelling at each other, but at some point, they were going to settle it, and then we'd have to fight them. I didn't like our odds. Troy looked pretty strong, but he was smaller and younger than them. And me? I had just proven that I didn't have the heart to shove another human being off the ledge. We'd have a better chance if we could split up – Troy could hold them off until I escaped, and if I was as valuable to them as I seemed to be, they would then chase after me and leave him alone.

But the gap between me and the next section of the balcony was a good seven feet wide. I couldn't jump it, and without a ladder or something, I couldn't—

Wait a minute.

"Your hoe," I told Troy. "Would it fit across that gap?"

"Seems like as good an idea as any," he said. He

held it out, and the other end just reached. He lowered the handle onto the bit of stone in front of us, then crouched down to hold it steady.

"Good luck," he said.

I wanted to take a few moments to work up my nerve, but I could see Longface Lucky copying our idea, laying down his hoe to cross towards us. So with no further nerve-working-up, I turned around and put my right foot on Troy's hoe.

Then I put my left foot on it, and just like that, I was standing several storeys above the ground on nothing but an overgrown garden implement.

But I was not going to look down. I was not. *I was not going to look down.*

On the plus side, the building wasn't shaking itself apart any more, and even though lots of it was now on the floor, there was still more-or-less a ceiling over our head. Maybe that last rumble was like the death shudder of whatever forces I'd unleashed with my lie. So the hoe was perfectly still, and Newfangled Troy was going to hold it tight, and I was going to be absolutely fine as long as I kept moving and didn't look down, and why was I standing there talking to myself instead of moving?

I lifted my right foot up slowly.

I moved it forwards, slowly.

I put it down in front of my left foot, slowly.
I lifted up my left foot, slowly.
Right foot.
Left foot.
I was not going to look down.
Right foot.
Left foot.
Right foot.
I was not going to look down.

CHAPTER 15

*R*ough voices called from behind me. "Oi there, missy! You be careful, now. You ain't nearly as valuable to us dead as alive."

"Although dead, you ain't a bad catch, neither, if you see what I mean."

I was not going to look back.

Right foot.

Left foot.

Right foot.

Out of the corner of my eye, something caught my attention. I glanced over and saw that I was in front of one of the previously blank windows, but it wasn't blank any more. It showed a half-completed image of me balancing on the hoe. As I took a step forwards, the image filled in just a little more. *Don't pay any attention to it*, I thought. *Don't get distracted.*

Right foot—

Wrong foot. I slammed it back down and wobbled. I threw out my arms and waved them wildly, but I was lurching from side to side and I couldn't get my balance. Three more seconds, and I was going to topple over.

That meant I had three seconds to get off this stupid hoe.

I ran forwards as lightly as I could, arms flapping like a baby bird on its first flight, and I just made it to the other side before I tumbled forwards. I landed on the walkway, my momentum rolling me over onto my back.

Above me, the window was now completed, with a dramatic image of me dashing along the hoe. I guess I was now part of the history of this building.

I didn't have much time to admire it, though. Richard the Raker and Longface Lucky were still balancing their way across the gap, but they were nearly at Troy's perch. Troy winked at me, picked up his hoe, and swung it around.

Longface and Richard ducked under Troy's first swing and leapt over his second. They managed to land nimbly both times, but it did force them to stop walking forwards.

"Oi there, boy, what's gotten into you?" Longface shouted.

"Sorry, gents," Troy said, swinging again. "I've been captivated by her beauty and charm."

Look, I don't know how magic works. Maybe after a big magical catastrophe like the one I had triggered, there's some kind of recharging period, where you can lie and get away with it. Who could say?

All I know is, when Troy said he had been captivated by me, the ceiling didn't collapse.

Unfortunately, I didn't know how much longer he could hold out, so there wasn't time to ask him about it. I ran on, through the archway Lady Roslyn had vanished into a few minutes ago.

Just inside it was another flight of stone stairs. This one was much shorter – or maybe it just seemed that way, since you can climb stairs a lot more quickly when the building isn't trying to kill you.

At the top was a doorway. I ran through it and slammed it behind me. There was a lock on the door, so I locked it, then looked to see where I was.

The room was an octagon, with no decorations except for a Victorian drinking fountain in the middle. Something about the room's low iron ceiling looked familiar, but what caught my attention was Lady Roslyn. She was slumped on the floor, unconscious, with a broken brick lying next to her. It looked like a piece of the wall had fallen off and hit her head.

"Lady Roslyn? Hello?" I tapped her shoulder, but she didn't wake up. I didn't see any blood, and her breathing seemed normal, so (I hoped) she wasn't too badly hurt. Probably she'd wake up soon. Until then, I was on my own.

I looked around and realized why the ceiling looked so familiar: it looked like a giant manhole cover. And that drinking fountain was just like the one I had seen outside the shopping arcade, right before we jumped into the sewer. It was the exact same set-up – only this time, the manhole cover was above the fountain.

Well, if it had worked before…

I closed my eyes and remembered that night at the family reunion when Aunt Uta had sung me to sleep. And then I began to run in a tight circle around the little room, whistling as best I could.

In the arcade, I had opened an umbrella first. But if I did that now, the drop of water would escape. Fortunately, based on the glowing water I had seen through the cathedral windows, the whole building was bathed in the same magic as the umbrella. I hoped that would be enough.

And it seemed to be, because as I whistled and

ran, the water started welling up from the fountain. At first, it was a little burble, and then it was a gentle line, and soon it became a blast that ploughed into the iron ceiling and quickly erased it.

With the iron gone, I could now see a much higher stone ceiling beyond it. I wasn't in a tiny room after all. I was at the base of a tall tower. Huge rusting bells hung high above me, with mouldy ropes dropping down almost close enough for me to reach. I jumped up, trying to grab one, but I couldn't quite make it. Halfway up the wall, between me and the bells, I saw a door built into the wall, but a fat lot of good it did me there.

I realized that my feet must have dried off at some point. And the reason I realized this was, they suddenly felt wet again. I looked down and saw that, having erased the ceiling, the water was now pooling on the floor. I wasn't whistling or running any more, but the fountain was still shooting out water.

In fact, it was shooting out more and more all the time, and the room was beginning to fill up. The water was already up to my ankles.

Great.

Over by the wall, as the cold water lapped over her legs, Lady Roslyn moaned a bit, then slowly woke up. By the time she had finished blinking and shaking her head, the water was already up to her shoulders, which woke her up completely. She leapt to her feet.

Now the water was up to my shoulders, and now my chin. Before it could reach my mouth, I started paddling, and so did Lady Roslyn. We floated up, up, up, as the tide rose towards the rusting bells. I could easily reach the ropes now, but there wasn't any need to grab them – the water was lifting me up more quickly than I could have pulled myself. In a moment, I was as high as the door in the wall, but before I could open it, the current swept me upwards.

Within seconds, it had lifted us up to the very ceiling, and it was still going, filling in the rapidly narrowing band of remaining air. I tilted my mouth up and frantically breathed in a last few gulps – and then there was nothing left to breathe.

Fortunately, the glow from the umbrella still lit up the water. I pointed to the door in the wall, which was now below us. Lady Roslyn nodded, and we both swam downwards.

When we got close enough, I reached out and grabbed the door handle and tried to turn it. It wouldn't budge. It must have rusted shut.

I gestured to Lady Roslyn, who grabbed it as well. We each braced ourselves with our free hands on the wall and yanked frantically on the handle. The gulp of air I had taken was running out. I desperately needed to breathe, but the handle wouldn't turn –

– and then it did. The door swung open, and water started gushing into it.

We gushed into it, too. Then we gushed out the other side.

For a moment, I shot through the air.

Then my face scraped to a stop on paved ground. I coughed out water, and I breathed in sweet-smelling night air. At long last, I was above ground.

When my lungs stopped complaining, I sat up and looked around. It was dark out, but there were enough streetlamps for me to see where I was.

I was lying between two parked cars in the middle of the parking lot in front of Charing Cross station.

I had been to the station before, and I had seen the tall stone monument next to the parking lot. But I had always assumed it was just … well, just a tall stone monument. Now that we had shot out of a door in its side, I realized I had underestimated it. It was actually the bell tower of a massive underground cathedral dedicated to a magical river – the only part of that cathedral that poked out above ground.

Well, boil me in Betty.

As I watched, the last bit of water gushed out of the door in the side of the monument and the door swung shut. From the outside, it didn't look like a door at all. It was just another stone panel on the side of the monument.

We sat there on the ground, enjoying the experience of being able to breathe. Plus, the clean water inside the bell tower had washed us off, mostly. It was nice not to smell like something unmentionable.

I took the moment to ask Lady Roslyn about something that had been bothering me. We had been a little too busy with the whole not-getting-crushed-by-a-cathedral thing for me to ask before now.

"Why shouldn't you lie around magic?"

By way of answer, she cocked an eyebrow at me.

"OK, yes," I said. "I saw what happened. But *why* did it happen?"

"Certain beings are so powerful, they can control magic with nothing more than their very will. The rest of us, when we can control it at all, must use words and pictures. And words and pictures are merely representations of reality. When we lie, we break the relationship between our words and our beliefs about reality, and the results can be" – she rubbed the bruise on her head – "unpleasant."

Now I understood why she had phrased things so carefully when she had been speaking to Long-face Lucky – "going around the glasshouse", as he had called it. She didn't want to tell him the full truth, but she didn't dare tell an outright lie. And that brought up another question.

"Why did those people think I was a – what did they call it? A tosheroon?"

"Every once in a while – once or twice a century, perhaps – the energy of the rivers fuses several powerful items into one item whose power is even greater than the sum of its parts. Bazalgette's Trowel is one such. It was found at the very source of the Tyburn River and used in the ceremonies that bound the rivers' powers underground. It vanished shortly thereafter."

That was so much to chew over that I almost didn't notice that she hadn't answered my question. "OK, but why did they think *I'm* a tosheroon?"

She sighed. "I'm not a mind reader, Hyacinth. I wouldn't dare guess what goes on inside Longface Lucky's unnaturally tall skull."

From a few blocks away, a church bell began tolling the time. I counted the strokes: eleven o'clock. There was one hour until that midnight deadline.

Lady Roslyn stood up. "Come," she said. "We have an appointment with some monsters, and we haven't much time."

PART
TWO

CHAPTER 16

I had faced down a giant angry pig. I had escaped a collapsing underground cathedral. I had avoided being captured by scavengers. All that was just a prelude to the one insurmountable challenge of the day:

Post office closing hours.

Lady Roslyn and I stood on the deserted street, looking through the darkened windows. There was nobody inside.

"Don't you have late-night post offices here?" I asked.

"I'm afraid we cling to the rather quaint notion that even postal workers ought to go home to their families on occasion."

"Then what are we supposed to do?"

"I have done and experienced much in my long life," Lady Roslyn said. "But I have never been so careless as to lose my own mother. I am at precisely as much of a loss as you."

I ignored the dig, and I thought about what I knew. What had the Saltpetre Men told me to do? They had said to report to the nearest post office once I had the drop of water. Then they had driven away with my mom—

No, wait. Before they drove off, they threw something at me.

I dug in my pocket, and despite all the rips in my jeans, and despite all the times I had been turned upside down and shaken around, the antique penny was still there. But what was I supposed to do with it?

Built into the wall of the building was a stamp-dispensing machine. There was nothing else for me to do, so I slid the penny into the coin slot.

The machine *click*ed, and an antique one-penny stamp slid out. I took it.

"Well done," said Lady Roslyn. "If we find ourselves in the early nineteenth century, we shall be able to send a postcard."

I'm sure I would have been able to come up with a really brilliant response to that, but fortunately, I didn't have to. There was another *click*, and the machine, and the wall around it, swung open.

Behind it was some kind of giant tube, curving back into a hole. From inside the tube came a loud *whoosh*.

I felt like I had seen that whole set-up before, in one of my history books, but I couldn't place it until a giant glass box, shaped like a huge pill, came hurtling out of the tube and landed with a *thunk*. Then I remembered. "That's a pneumatic tube. They used to use them at banks, only those were smaller. You'd put a message in the glass box and put the glass box in the big vacuum tube, and it would get sucked up and shot off to whoever the message was for."

The door of the giant glass box swung open. It was cushioned inside, and it looked like there was just enough room for us both to squeeze in. It didn't exactly look comfortable.

But what alternative did we have? I looked at Lady Roslyn. She looked at me.

We climbed in, and the door swung shut behind us. Then, with a mighty *whoosh*, the glass box, and us with it, got sucked upwards.

Over the past couple of hours, I had been hurtled up and down through enough dark passages that I would have thought I'd get used to it. But having my cheek pressed up against Lady Roslyn's, with a glowing umbrella wedged between us, added a whole new level of oh-my-God-I-hope-I-don't-vomit to the experience.

Plus, the giant glass pill kept slowly turning around as it shot through the pneumatic tube, so first I'd fall onto Lady Roslyn, then she'd fall onto me, and then we'd repeat. (On the plus side, the water never leaked out of the umbrella, despite the tossing. I guess there was some kind of magic force field keeping it in.)

"I have noticed," Lady Roslyn said as we toppled back and forth, "that young people are particularly – OOF! – susceptible to fads. In my youth, for example, there was one of bright red lipstick. I mention this because – OUCH! – now that we're face to face, I'm curious to know if leaving your teeth unbrushed has become suddenly fashionable."

As crazy as my mom and dad were about a lot of things (like whether macaroni belonged in pancakes, or whether moms and dads belonged together), they had brought me up pretty well, and I knew it was wrong to insult an elderly woman. Which meant I couldn't say about 99 per cent of the things I wanted to say when Lady Roslyn insulted *me*. I just bit my tongue, metaphorically.

And then I bit my tongue literally. I also bit both cheeks and a lip, because the glass box came to the end of the pneumatic tube and crashed into the floor with teeth-clattering force.

The box swung open, and we staggered out.

We were in a room that hadn't been dusted in half a century. It must have been some sort of arrival hall. In a row along one wall were the open ends of a dozen different pneumatic tubes. There was leather padding on the floor, probably to make for a soft landing, but it was tattered, with only a few bits of stuffing left. No wonder we had landed with such a loud crash.

Old propaganda posters clung to the wall. One of them showed two men fighting each other next to a glowing underground river, while a big image of a soldier wearing a spiky helmet loomed over them, rubbing his hands in glee. The caption said, WHEN WE FIGHT EACH OTHER, THE KAISER WINS. Another poster showed a burning building, with the caption DID THE GERMANS DO THIS? OR DID YOU MIX HOT AND COLD WATER?

Lady Roslyn looked around and sighed. "One might imagine that when the Royal Mail's budget was cut, it would siphon money from its less important functions, like delivering the mail. One might hope that the facilities for preventing magical catastrophe would be updated regularly. Sadly, one would be wrong."

A group of dusty, burned-out light bulbs was arranged in an arrow, pointing out the door. We followed them and headed down a long corridor, lit by a few flickering fluorescent lights.

The corridor opened out onto a road, and on the side of the road was a post office. It looked exactly like the post office outside of which we had entered the pneumatic tube, but with two key differences.

First, it was clearly open. Through the dirty windows, we could make out a line of people waiting inside.

And second, it was underground. Instead of the night sky above us, there was a jagged rock ceiling. The road in front of it wasn't more than twenty feet long, and it led from one jagged rock wall to another.

We crossed the road, opened the door, and stepped in, and took our place at the end of the line. There were two dozen people ahead of us, all clutching parcels and envelopes. And the parcels were all glowing, or trembling, or rumbling ominously. From inside one of them, a muffled voice was calling out, "I say! A fellow can't see in here! Who turned out all the lights?"

Now that I looked closely, not all the people were actually people. A number of places ahead of us was a Saltpetre Man, calmly holding a ukulele that was frantically playing itself.

Just like in an above ground post office, there were long counters, with clerks standing behind Plexiglas windows. These clerks, though, weren't human; they were Saltpetre Men. The monsters weren't any faster-moving down here than they had been when we had run away from them before. That explained why the line was moving so slowly, but it raised another question.

"If the Saltpetre Men work here, why is that one waiting in line with everybody else?" I asked.

"Presumably because he is here in his off hours, rather than in his capacity as an employee of the Royal Mail."

"But why does the Royal Mail hire monsters in the first place? What does the mail have to do with the secret rivers?"

"Ah, it's taken you a mere thirteen hours to ask that. No doubt you arrived at it so quickly thanks to all the time your generation saves by not working hard at anything."

Fine. I wasn't going to insult her back, but maybe I could borrow her trick and dance right up to the edge of insulting her without technically crossing over. "So is dodging questions something *your* generation is good at, or is that just you?"

She looked pleased. "You do have the tiniest bit of spirit after all! My dear, you don't know how happy that makes me. If I seem hard on you at times, it is simply because you're about a hard business. I'm hoping all my little digs will let you build up a thick skin, for when you have to face genuine horror."

I tried to imagine what the genuine horror she was preparing me for was, but then I realized: "You did it again. You still haven't answered my question."

She smiled again. "Well spotted. When magic is around, no one will dare lie to you, but many will do everything they can to dodge the truth. Now, then. The Royal Mail hires monsters as the result of a century-old compromise. I've already told you that there is a demented faction of anarchists that wishes to see the power of the rivers handed out like candy. That faction has cells around the world – in Paris, and New York, and Tokyo, and anywhere there are similar sources of magical power. In 1914, one of those foreign cells assassinated Archduke Franz Ferdinand of Austria. I don't wish to presume too much historical knowledge on your part, since you are an American, but you may have heard of the consequence of that assassination: a little disagreement known as World War One.

"Now, were I in charge of the government, I might have responded by crushing the British branch of the anarchist cult that started the war. Then, heeding the wisdom of the Inheritors of Order, I would have forbidden the use of magic by all but a specially trained elite. However, our democratically elected representatives chose a different path. They shut down *all* sides in the fight over the rivers' power. They imposed a truce, buttressed by a series of compromises. For example, hot and cold water could be mixed in the shower, since shower heads break the water up into lots of tiny little streams, which diminishes their power to a small, safe dose. Anybody who took a shower in the proximity of a secret river would get a modest boost of inspiration, without risking another Great Fire."

"OK, this whole hot and cold water thing. Even with the dumb sink in my aunt's flat, they mix in the basin. Why isn't that a problem?"

Lady Roslyn looked at me as if this were the most ludicrous question in the world. "Because it's an open space, of course. The magic can't reach critical mass unless it's confined. Now, where was I? Ah, yes: the shameful compromise. The anarchists felt it did not go far enough. The Inheritors of Order felt it went too far. But both sides agreed to it because Britain was at war with Germany, and everybody was willing to put aside their differences for the national good.

"Of course, when the war ended, the government didn't want to let go of the power it had acquired. It continued to enforce the truce. When anybody got their hands on a particularly significant magical item, the government swept in and confiscated it, lest it give an advantage to one side or the other. And this drop of water" – she hefted the umbrella – "would be a significant advantage indeed."

"But why the *post office*?"

"Partly because the Royal Mail was already in charge of the telegraph system, so they had experience in dealing with lines of power running underground. Partly because they had branches and employees (and, therefore, eyes and ears) all over the city. But mostly because, in the entire history of humanity, nobody has ever assassinated an archduke in the name of lower postal rates. And their strategy worked. In the century since, most people have forgotten the very existence of the magical rivers, and those few who remember don't do much about it. Thus was the most important and noble cause in human history reduced to an endless series of bureaucratic quibbles."

The Saltpetre Man had finally made it to the front of the queue. He shuffled up to the service window and put the self-playing ukulele through a Plexiglas door. The worker on the other side of the window pulled a lever. The Plexiglas door swung shut, and another door on the inside swung open.

I had seen the same security system in regular, above ground post offices. There, it was to prevent somebody from sticking a gun in the clerk's face and pulling off a robbery. I wondered what it was meant to prevent here.

I had a long time to think about it. It turns out that in England, epic magical quests involve an awful lot of standing in queues.

One by one, the people ahead of us turned in their magic items. Some of them got things back in exchange, although nobody seemed to get back their lost parents. (Except maybe the Saltpetre Man. After he gave up the ukulele, he got back an urn full of dirt. He hugged it so happily that it definitely could have been his mom.)

Finally, it was our turn. Up close, the Saltpetre Man behind the counter turned out to be a Saltpetre Woman. At least, it was wearing makeup and a flowered cap, although it had the same shapeless shape and Royal Mail uniform. When it opened its lipsticked mouth, it spoke in the same unisex gurgle as the other creatures. "How may I provide you with exsssellent sssservisse today?"

"I'd like to exchange this umbrella for my mom," I said.

I slid the umbrella through the Plexiglas door. Just as the Saltpetre Woman swung it shut, Lady Roslyn leaned forwards and whispered something to the umbrella. Yes, that's what I said: she whispered to the umbrella. I couldn't quite hear for certain, but it sounded like she was saying, "My name is Lady Rosamond. I am one hundred and sixty-eight centimetres tall."

"What did you—" I started to ask, but Lady Roslyn gave a quick shake of her head, which I figured was her way of telling me to shut up.

On the other side of the window, the Saltpetre Woman picked up the umbrella. It was starting to tremble a little, and I realized what Lady Roslyn had done. She had lied to it. At least, the thing about her name was definitely a lie, and I was willing to bet the thing about her height was, too.

I wasn't sure why, after everything she had told me, Lady Roslyn had suddenly decided that lying when magic was around would be a good idea. Still, they weren't especially big lies. Maybe they wouldn't have very big consequences.

The Saltpetre Woman apparently didn't notice that the umbrella was shaking, because she just slid it into a glass cylinder and put it into the pneumatic tube. As it rose up, the shaking of the umbrella finally made the glass cylinder vibrate hard enough for the Saltpetre Woman to notice it. She reached out to grab it, but she was far too slow, and the cylinder got sucked up out of sight.

It must have been shaking harder and harder as it

went, because I could hear it thumping around inside the pneumatic tube, louder and louder, as it rose.

As the thumps turned into bangs, Lady Roslyn leaned over and whispered a single word to me: "Duck." She crouched down next to the counter. I didn't need to be told twice – I crouched down next to her.

And just in time, too, because, from inside the pneumatic tube, the umbrella suddenly burst open with a *BANG!* The pneumatic tube flew into pieces, and dozens of flying bits of iron crashed into the Plexiglas safety window, shattering it.

The other customers screamed.

The Saltpetre clerks staggered backwards.

The umbrella hung there in the air, spinning around, with the drop of water hovering in the middle like a fiery red bowling ball.

Then Lady Roslyn, in one swift motion, leapt up, jumped through the jagged hole in the Plexiglas, grabbed the umbrella in mid-air, closed it over the giant glowing drop, and landed on the floor on the other side.

She glanced back over her shoulder at me. "Well, are you coming or not?" she asked. Then she ran through a door and vanished.

CHAPTER 17

*J*climbed over the counter and ran after her. What else could I do?

Then I ran through the door. In the hallway beyond it, I managed to catch up to Lady Roslyn. "Why did you do that?" I demanded. "They were about to give me my mother back."

"What makes you so sure?"

"Well, obviously, they – I mean, I'm sure— Fine. What about all those people? They could have gotten hurt."

"But *did* they?"

"I don't know! You didn't give me the chance to look!"

From behind us, a voice called, "Sssstop, pleasssse.

You are tressssspassssing." More voices joined in, repeating that last word: "Tressssspassssing. Tressssspassssing." I wasn't going to make the mistake of looking over my shoulder, but I could tell there were at least half a dozen Saltpetre Men behind us.

"They'll never catch up with us," Lady Roslyn said as we went through the door at the end of the hallway.

We were in a huge room – it looked like some kind of big mail sorting facility. Dozens of Saltpetre Men were working there. Some of them were tossing parcels into wheeled carts, and others were pushing the carts around, and still others were taking the parcels out and feeding them into giant, clanking machines. Then the machines spat the parcels out onto one of the hundreds of conveyor belts that ran in all directions, from the floor up to the ceiling.

From somewhere, an alarm went, "AOOOGAH! AOOOGAH!" and a voice over an intercom said, "Tressssspasssssersssss… Tressssspasssssersssss… Tressssspasssssersssss…"

Immediately, every Saltpetre Man in that huge room turned towards us and joined in the chorus: "Tressssspasssssersssss… Tressssspasssssersssss…"

They started to shuffle towards us. "Tressssspasssssersssss…"

And from the corridor behind us, I could hear

more voices saying the same thing, getting closer and closer.

"Follow me," said Lady Roslyn. She grabbed one of the wheeled carts, ran forwards with it for a few steps, and jumped in. I managed to jump in just behind her.

"Tressssspasssssserssss... Tressssspasssssserssss..."

The cart shot forwards, right between two of the monsters, and Lady Roslyn jumped back out again. She landed nimbly on one of the machines. I tried to do the same thing but missed the machine and landed on the floor.

I climbed up next to her, a little clumsily. As usual, she didn't show the slightest sign of being out of breath. "How old are you again?" I asked her.

Instead of answering, Lady Roslyn pointed inside the machine. There were little wooden shelves spaced a few feet apart along a conveyor belt, and a panel that swung shut, then open, then shut again, every time one of the shelves passed by.

"Um," I said. "You don't seriously think we're going to—"

Before I could finish, the panel flipped open, and Lady Roslyn dove forwards and slipped through it just before it closed again.

"Oh, boy," I said. The panel flipped open again, and before I could think too hard about it, I leapt.

I almost made it, but the panel started to close just before I made it all the way through, and it slammed shut on my ankle.

"Ow!" I said, yanking my foot out. But Lady Roslyn was already two feet above my head, because the conveyor belt started heading straight up as soon as it came out of the machine.

"Are you coming or not?" she called down to me.

"Tressssspasssssersssss… Tressssspasssssersssss…"

I didn't have much choice. I balanced as best I could on the shallow wooden shelf and let it carry me up.

And up, and up, and up, through a forest of belts and pipes, until we were almost at the high ceiling. We passed a narrow metal catwalk, and Lady Roslyn stepped off onto it, as casually as if she were stepping down off a bus. I tried to do the same thing, but in the few seconds it took me to work up my nerve, the conveyor belt carried me a little too high, and I misjudged the distance, and my foot slammed down on the catwalk, and it turned out that the catwalk was hanging from chains instead of fixed to the wall. It swung out from under me and I almost went plummeting down to the ground.

I grabbed the handrail tightly as the catwalk swung wildly back and forth.

"I'm sure you're relatively lovely," Lady Roslyn said

calmly. "Nevertheless, you would not be my first choice for the last sight I ever see. Do try not to send me plummeting to my doom."

I looked down past the tangle of conveyor belts stretching to the floor, where the crowd of monsters looked back up at me, all chanting that single hissing word: "Tressssspasssssersssss… Tressssspasssssersssss…"

Then I turned back to Lady Roslyn. "So where's my mom?"

"I was going to ask you the same question."

"WHAT?? After dragging me through the sewers – and blowing up the post office when they might have just given her back – how on earth can you—"

She put a gentle hand on my shoulder. "Your mother is somewhere nearby, Hyacinth, and nobody is better qualified than you to determine exactly where. Close your eyes. Which way should we go?"

I took a deep breath and closed my eyes. I wasn't exactly sure how I was supposed to do this, but I tried to sense where Mom was. It was no use. All I could sense was the chanting of the Saltpetre Men below, and the pain in my ankle, and a conveyor belt that I really needed to get onto, and a cramp in my—

Wait a minute. What was that about a conveyor belt? I opened my eyes and pointed to it. "That one. We have to get on that one."

This time, I led the way. I jumped off the catwalk and onto a conveyor belt that took me down to another conveyor belt that took me over to another conveyor belt that took me up to *exactly the right conveyor belt.*

I don't know how I knew. All I knew, as it lifted me out of the room and into a vent in the ceiling, was that I was closer to my mom than I had been since the monsters took her away.

CHAPTER 18

$\mathcal{J}$ust past the vent, the conveyor belt twisted around suddenly, dumping us off. We fell into a dimly lit room.

We landed on a big pile of musty old scrolls – one of many that filled the room. Some of the scrolls were glowing, which, I realized, was where the room's dim light came from. There were no bulbs overhead.

There were also no doors. The only way out was via the conveyor belt, now a good seven feet above our heads.

Lady Roslyn looked around. "Excellent work," she said. "Apparently, your mother is some sort of rolled-up piece of paper."

I ignored her, which was a skill I was getting plenty of practice in. Instead, I started to dig through one of the piles of scrolls. I don't know how I knew it was the right place to start – I just *knew*.

I lifted up one of the scrolls and found a finger. I jumped, because I knew exactly whose finger it was. The ring on it still had the scratches from when I was four and Mom had made the mistake of telling me that the engraving on the ring was a bay leaf, like Grandma used in her recipes. The next morning, I had taken the ring from Mom's night table, dropped it into the blender, and tried to make soup. It had survived, more or less, and Mom was completely forgiving about it. (Which, I have to admit, she always was about everything.) "Don't worry about the scratches," she had told me cheerfully as she put it back on. "That just gives it some extra history."

Seeing my mom's finger in the pile of scrolls, I had a moment of panic, until I pulled off more scrolls and discovered that the finger was still attached to her hand, which was still attached to her arm, which was still attached to...

"Mom!" I said as I frantically knocked away the scrolls. I was relieved to see that she was still breathing, and she didn't seem to have been hurt. But she didn't respond when I shook her shoulders and said, "Mom! Wake up! It's Hyacinth!"

Lady Roslyn pulled me away. "That's not going

to work. It's an enchanted sleep. Waking her will be simple when the time is right."

"What are we waiting for, then?"

"Do you think having your mother awake will be a help in a complex and dangerous situation, or a hindrance?"

OK, she had a point. Mom always reacted calmly when I screwed something up, but any other unexpected circumstance in life threw her into a tizzy. I had seen her react to a lost shoe like it was a major military catastrophe. I wasn't sure how she'd deal with being woken up in the middle of a magical sorting facility full of lumbering, glittery-eyed monsters.

Lady Roslyn looked at me kneeling next to my mom. "Stay like that," she said, and leapt onto my shoulders.

"Ow," I said.

"Stop talking," Lady Roslyn said. "It makes it hard to maintain my balance."

"Then stop digging your heels into my— Ow!"

Lady Roslyn stretched her arms up, but even perched on me, she couldn't reach the conveyor belt. "Stand up," she said.

"Are you kidding me?"

"Do you want to get out of here or not? Put your hands on my ankles to hold me on your shoulders, then stand up."

The putting-my-hands-on-her-ankles part was pretty easy. The standing up part wasn't, but I staggered to my feet, feeling like I was in the worst circus act ever. But somehow I managed to stay upright.

Lady Roslyn stretched out her arms until she could reach the conveyor belt. She pulled herself up onto it, then balanced carefully, one leg on either side of the moving bit, so she could stand in place. "Now pass your mother up," she said.

It's true my mom was pretty small for a grown-up. But I had never tried lifting her above my head. Still, I wasn't sure how else we were going to get out of there, so I bent back down and picked her up.

Holy moly, my mother was heavy.

With a lot of grunting, I managed to get her up to my waist. With even more grunting, I managed to raise her up to my chest, but that was as high as I could lift her.

Lady Roslyn knelt down, still keeping one leg on either side of the moving walkway, and stretched her arms down. She couldn't quite reach Mom. "Lift her higher."

Easy for her to say. I tried with all my might, but I just couldn't get Mom above my head. At least, I couldn't get *all* of her. So I flopped her arms up, and Lady Roslyn managed to grab them. Finally, she pulled

Mom off the ground and up onto the conveyor belt.

"Excellent," Lady Roslyn said. "Well done." She slung Mom over her shoulders and stepped onto the moving part of the conveyor belt.

"Hey!" I yelled. "How do *I* get up there?"

Lady Roslyn lifted up her hand, and, without even looking back at me, gave a little wave as the conveyor belt carried her out of sight.

"HEY!!" I yelled.

No answer.

And then another alarm began hooting and a red light started flashing from somewhere. "Intruder in the ssscroll room," a voice boomed. "Intruder in the ssscroll room."

I heard a hissing noise on top of the alarm, and the room started to fill with a milky-white gas.

I grabbed one of the scrolls and pressed it over my face. It didn't help. Everything started to fade away.

The last thing I saw before I passed out was the faded words on the ancient paper I had grabbed: *This scrolle is notte to be usyd as protechsynne agÿnst ye gaseousse fumes.*

Oh, well, I thought. Everything went black.

CHAPTER 19

The hissing was still there, but it somehow sounded fainter and gentler.

I was in thick darkness.

No, it wasn't darkness. My eyes were closed. And it felt good, probably because it was the first rest I had gotten since I woke up on my last ordinary, non-magical day. Finally, I convinced myself to open them.

I was in a narrow room with stained floors and a low ceiling made out of chipped and dank stone. I was handcuffed to an ancient iron chair, and in one corner, a humidifier hissed out mist. A rusting iron lever stuck out of the floor – but other than that, the room was empty.

The door opened, and a Saltpetre Man shuffled in.

"Why?" he asked.

"Why what?" I asked.

"Why ssssteal?"

Maybe I was still a little loopy from the gas, but I had no idea what he was getting at. "You mean, why does anybody steal, in general? No, wait. You mean, why steal my mom back?"

He nodded. "Why ssssteal?"

"I didn't steal her. Lady Roslyn did. And anyway, if I had stolen her, it wouldn't be stealing. She's *my mom*."

"Why ssssteal?"

We weren't getting anywhere. Now, I didn't know the first thing about how magic worked here in London, but my dad had taught me seven magic words that often got things done back home. So I tried saying them now: "May I please speak to your supervisor?"

"Ssssupervisssor?" The monster thought it over, which was clearly a slow process. Then he shuffled out and closed the door behind him.

"Hey! Where'd you go? Come back! Hey!"

Silence.

It must have been a good ten minutes before the door opened again and another Saltpetre Man stumbled in. This one seemed a little different from the others. For one thing, his Royal Mail uniform had epaulets on the shoulders, like a military uniform. For another, he had the fastest shuffle I had seen. It was like somebody had filmed one of the other monsters and then played it back at double speed.

"Good morning, misss," he said. "Inssspector Ssandss, Royal Mail Polisse Forsse." The hiss in his voice was unmistakable but much gentler than the other Saltpetre Men's.

He offered me his hand. I shook it with my un-handcuffed hand and tried not to make a face – it felt like squeezing a full nappy.

"Before you sspeak," he continued, "I musst warn you that the room is being moissturiszed with en-chanted river water." He gestured to the humidifier. "Your lungss are full of it. I do not advisze you to lie."

Did that mean he had to tell the truth, too? Did he even have lungs?

I said, "That other thing I spoke to—" Then I stopped myself, because I wasn't sure if he'd be of-fended by being called a thing. I corrected myself, just to be safe. "I mean, your coworker – I don't think I understood what he wanted to ask me."

"You were in the prossess of returning the re-quessted magical item. All you had to do wass await your mother'ss return. Why causse uss all sso much trouble?"

Honestly, I was wondering the same thing myself.

A lot of the things Lady Roslyn had done had seemed crazy at the time, but they had all ended up making sense – even jumping into the sewer. But I couldn't figure out why she hadn't just handed over the umbrella and let me get Mom.

Still, she had come back for me before, rescuing me from Little Ben just in the nick of time. Surely she'd come back and get me out of this situation, and I could demand explanations then.

In the meantime, I wasn't going to give any answers to one of the creatures that had kidnapped my mom. Instead, I took a page from Lady Roslyn's book, and changed the subject. "Where am I?" I asked.

"You are in the Mount Pleassant Mail Ssorting Fassility, medium ssecurity division."

Oh. That didn't sound good. Maybe I should change away from *that* subject, too. "You're the first Saltpetre Man I've heard speak in complete sentences."

"I have an advantage over the otherss," he said, and took off his cap. For a moment, I thought he was just making a polite gesture. Then I realized that the top of his skull had come off with his hat. He tilted his head forwards so I could look inside his head.

"It's *empty*!" I exclaimed.

"Better empty than full of mud," he said. "Indeed, I have ssometimess found an empty head to be better than a human brain." He plopped the cap, and the top of his skull, back into place. "Now, if you've finisshed dodging my quesstion, perhapss you can ansswer it."

Maybe I wasn't as good as Lady Roslyn at dodging questions after all. I didn't know what else to say, so I just sat there in silence.

Finally, Inspector Sands gave a disappointed sigh.

"Very well, misss. You leave me no choisse." He pulled the rusty lever that I had noticed sticking out of the floor. Immediately the hissing of the humidifier was drowned out by the thunderous rumble of stone moving over stone. All four walls began to slide slowly down into the floor.

And meanwhile, the iron chair I was handcuffed to started to twist and unfold and stretch out. As it straightened, I had to stand up if I didn't want to fall to the floor. I wondered if it was going to end up as some kind of torture device. My hand trembled in the handcuff.

But the iron chair wasn't turning into a rack or an iron maiden. When it had finished flipping around, it had turned into a Victorian version of the treadmill my dad used to exercise on. The leather that had been the seat was now under my feet, and it started to move, forcing me to walk fast to keep up.

By now, the walls had slid down into the floor, and I could see that my little cell had just been a blocked-off part of a much bigger room, made of the same dank stone. There were two dozen other treadmills there, all arranged in rows. A few of them were empty, but most of them had other prisoners handcuffed to them, all walking in place.

Most of the other prisoners were human, although the faces of a bunch of them were hidden behind long dirty hair, or lots of scars, or both, so I couldn't be sure what they were.

Others were definitely *not* human. One of them, dressed in a tuxedo and top hat, had the head of a mosquito. Another was a massive white lion, three times as tall as I was, who looked like he had been carved out of some kind of living stone. There was even a fairy on a teeny-tiny little treadmill.

And right next to me was a unicorn, chained to his treadmill by a golden collar around his neck. When I was little, I had loved reading about unicorns, and I had always dreamed I might meet one someday. Trust me: this was not the unicorn I had dreamed about. He had an unhinged look in his eyes, and the white hair on his chin was flecked with black, which made him look like some sleazy guy who had just woken up and hadn't bothered to shave. When I looked at him, he looked back at me with an intense stare that made me look away immediately.

I figured the safest thing to do was just point my eyes straight ahead so I would be looking at the back of the head of whoever was on the treadmill in front of me. The only problem was, the guy in front of me was wearing his head completely backwards, so even though his back was to me, we ended up making eye contact. He winked at me, which made him look even creepier, because his eyelids flicked in from the sides instead of the top and bottom.

"You can't leave me here!" I said to Inspector Sands.

"Oh, it'ss perfectly ssafe, asz long asz none of the other priszonerss break their chainss."

"Does that ever happen?"

"Rarely more than oncze a month. I sshall return sshortly to ssee whether you have reconssidered your ssilensse."

He's bluffing, I thought. *No way is he going to leave a twelve-year-old girl locked in here with all these—*

The door slammed behind him.

Maybe he wasn't bluffing after all.

Hello, little girl, the unicorn said. But he didn't actually say it. His lips didn't even move. The words just appeared inside my head.

"I'm not a little girl. I'm—"

Oh, I know exactly how old you are, Hyacinth Herkanopoulos. I know things about you that you don't even know yourself. And as soon as I get out of this chain, we're going to have all sorts of fun together.

I was about to tell him that Herkanopoulos was my mother's name, not mine, but I decided I didn't want to give him any more personal information than he already knew. Then I worried that just by thinking about it, I had.

"I don't know what you're telling her," the tuxedoed mosquito said, "but you better not be calling dibs. I'm going to want a piece of her, too. Save me the contents of her veins, and you can have the rest."

The other prisoners roared with laughter – all except for the giant stone lion, who roared with anger instead. "You yoinks! You rotters! You cads! Leave that, that, that poor girl alone or, or I'll – *hic!*" He cleared his throat with a hoarse roar and tried again. "I'll – *hic!*"

The others laughed even louder.

The lion turned its stone head towards me and gave me a friendly nod. "Young lady, don't let these – *hic!*" Even from a distance, his hiccup was powerful enough to send a gust of his breath towards me. It smelled like an entire bottle of Aunt Callie's favourite whisky. And now that I thought about it, he was weaving drunkenly as he walked along his treadmill. Even just turning his head towards me seemed to throw him off balance, forcing him to turn away with an apologetic look.

"Don't think he's any better than the rest of us," said the mosquito. "I bet he'd eat you, too, if he could keep solid food down."

"Liar! Hoodlum! *Hic! Hic!*"

I'm bored, the unicorn thought at me. *Let's make things more interesting.*

It pointed its horn away from me and towards Backwards Head. That must have been how it aimed its thoughts, since I couldn't hear it any more, but I did hear Backwards Head snickering. That couldn't be a good thing.

"Great idea," he said. And he and the unicorn started to walk faster.

As soon as they did, my own treadmill started to move faster under my feet. They must all have been linked together. I picked up my pace.

The unicorn pointed his horn back at me. *I want you nice and worn out, little girl. It'll give you that much less strength to fight back.* He twisted his neck at an angle I wouldn't have thought possible and stuck the tip of his horn into the lock of the chain around his neck. There was a *click*, and he giggled. *One pin down. Two to go. And then you're mine.*

I looked up at the lion. Could I count on him for help? No – he clearly had troubles of his own. Now that the treadmills were going faster, he was staggering even more.

Hmm. That gave me an idea. But I hated to do it – the lion was the only one there who had shown me any kindness.

Click. Two pins down. One to go.

There was no time to think about it any more. Sorry about that, drunk stone lion.

I pretended to stumble a little and said, "Don't make it go so fast! Please, I beg you! I can barely stand up!"

Backwards Head laughed and started to go even faster. Now I was jogging to keep up. "Oh, please stop!" I said, trying to sound as scared as possible (which wasn't actually too hard, under the circumstances). Just in case I was being too subtle, I added, "I can just barely keep up, as long as nobody else is running, but—"

That did the trick. The other prisoners started hooting and cheering – and running as fast as they could. The treadmill beneath my feet whirred frantically. The lion was starting to stumble over his own paws, but he had a kind of a drunken grace, and he somehow managed to catch himself each time.

Click. The lock on the unicorn's chain sprang open. He leered at me –

– and at that moment, the lion tumbled too heavily

to right himself. His paws shot out from under him and he crashed down onto his speeding treadmill, which shot him backwards so forcefully, his chain snapped.

He flew backwards, crashing into the unicorn and sending them both smashing into the hard stone wall.

Backwards Head looked horrified. "Sirion!" he called. "Sirion! Are you OK?"

The unicorn didn't answer.

In a few seconds, the other prisoners were going to realize what had just happened and stop running. That didn't leave me much time. I grabbed hold of my handcuffed wrist with my free hand, locked my knees, and leaned forwards.

The speeding treadmill shot me backwards. I felt like my arms were ripping out of their sockets, but I held on tight. The handcuffs bent. They didn't break.

"Stop running, you fools!" Backwards Head yelled. "She's trying to—"

But I had already pulled myself upright, and before he could finish, I shot myself backwards again. This time, the handcuffs snapped into pieces. I flew backwards, crashing into the wall. But unlike Sirion the unicorn, I had known it was coming, which meant I could cushion my fall, and stop myself from getting hurt ...

… much.

Ouch.

Ouch ouch ouch.

But at least I was conscious, and there was no time for moaning. I staggered to my feet.

The other prisoners had stopped running. They turned menacingly towards me – except for Backwards Head, of course, who didn't have to turn around to glare daggers at me. "Look what you did to Sirion's horn," he said.

I looked. The horn was hanging off the unicorn's head, held on only by a tiny thread of bone.

"You're going to pay for that," murmured Backwards Head. The other prisoners nodded agreement and started tugging on their chains, trying to break free.

Time to get out of here, I thought.

Dodging a series of smelly and/or hairy outstretched arms, I sprinted to the door and pulled madly.

It didn't open.

"That's a very solid door," said Backwards Head. "Too bad these handcuffs aren't so solid." He yanked on them with his massive arms. I could see them bending.

I pounded on the door. "Hey! Inspector Sands! I'll talk! You've got to get me out of here."

No answer.

Backwards Head gave his handcuffs one last mighty pull, and they shattered.

He smiled at me.

It was not a friendly smile.

CHAPTER 20

$\mathcal{J}$ pounded on the door again. The only response came from the prisoners, who stomped along, as if I were beating out the rhythm for some kind of demented chorus.

Not the reaction I was hoping for.

I looked over at the stone lion, but he was still slumped unconscious on top of the unicorn. I was on my own.

Backwards Head wobbled towards me. He was not exactly a graceful walker, since he had to walk backwards to see where he was going. Then he got close enough to grab me, which meant he had to turn around so that his arms were pointing in the right direction for grabbing. But that meant, of course, that he couldn't see *where* he was grabbing, so I ducked out of his reach easily.

I was just beginning to wonder what I had been so frightened of when somebody shoved me from behind and I went falling right into Backwards Head's arms. Backwards Head spun me around and held me tight, allowing me to see who had done the shoving.

It was the tuxedoed mosquito. He must have broken his chains while I was busy with Backwards Head. His long nose twitched, sniffing up and down my arm in a disgustingly ticklish way.

"I've been terribly rude," he said. "I haven't even introduced myself. Seeing how I'm going to be deep within your veins, you ought to at least know my name. Geoffrey Noctofimus, at your service."

"That's very kind," I said. "But I don't actually require any services at the moment."

His nose twitched higher, up towards my elbow. "Ah, but you do. You very much do. You see, those of you who dwell in London have a problem. You consume a small portion of magic with every glass of tap water, and the closer you live to one of the rivers, the larger that portion is. And *you* live right above a source, don't you? I can smell it on you. Too much magic – well, it's not good for anybody. So allow me to remove it for you."

I tried to break free, but Backwards Head was holding me too tightly. Geoffrey Noctofimus plunged his needlelike nose into my arm, and, although it didn't actually hurt, I screamed in surprise and disgust. He started slurping something out of me. I could see the clear, glowing fluid snorkelling up his snout. Whatever he was taking out of me, it wasn't blood.

When he spoke again, his voice was slurring a little bit, like he was getting drunk. "Now, then, that's better, isn't it?"

I tried to answer, but nothing came out of my mouth. Things were going grey. I mean, the prison hadn't exactly been the most colourful place I'd ever visited, but in the back of my mind, I could at least remember what lay outside. But as the fluid slid up his snout, I could feel everything interesting about the world slipping away. It was all dimming. Grandma's farm... Mom and Dad, dancing together before everything went bad... Aunt Rainey sitting on the porch...

Wait. That last one. There was something important about it. I let everything else slip away, but I grabbed on to that image with every bit of mental energy I had. And I remembered:

I'd been sitting on the porch with Aunt Rainey, and a mosquito had landed on her wrist. I would have swatted it, but Aunt Rainey just looked at it in her usual calm way. "Watch this," she had said, and she had bent her hand down so that the muscles in her wrist tightened. Its stinger trapped, the mosquito couldn't pull out. It swelled and swelled, and then it just kind of broke and Aunt Rainey's blood oozed out of it.

It would be crazy to try the same thing now. Who knew how much this giant mosquito-headed thing could suck up of whatever it was sucking?

But it was the only idea I had, and somehow I knew that if I didn't try it, I'd never have another idea again. So I tightened my muscles, just like Aunt Rainey had done. Having a giant mosquito in my arm had been disgusting enough, but holding it there added a whole other layer of yuck.

Fortunately, he didn't look like he was enjoying it, either. He tried to jerk back, but he was stuck. He tried to say something – probably to call for help – but the only thing that came out was a little suffocated gurgle.

My knees started to buckle, but I could see him getting more and more panicked. *I don't have to last for ever*, I thought. *I just have to last longer than him*. It was just a question of willpower. And now that he had sucked out all my imagination, willpower was all I had left.

His forehead was starting to bulge. At first, it was a

little bump the size of a pea, but it was growing.

All around me, the room was fading. If Backwards Head hadn't been holding me so tightly, I would have collapsed.

The bump in Geoffrey Noctofimus's head was now the size of a quarter. Then a hockey puck. And suddenly, his whole head puffed up like a blowfish, and then his arms and his legs and his shoulders did, too. The other prisoners finally realized something was wrong – I could hear them shouting, but everything sounded very far away to me.

And then Geoffrey Noctofimus exploded. Bits of mosquito brain and burning tuxedo went everywhere as an enormous ball of flame erupted out of his head and the rest of his body collapsed onto the floor.

The force of the explosion knocked Backwards Head backwards. Or maybe it knocked him forwards, depending on which way you looked at it. Either way, I went with him. As he slammed into the ground, his arms flung open, and I rolled free.

Meanwhile, the ball of flame that had exploded out of Geoffrey Noctofimus was zipping around the room as if looking for something. Then it spotted me and dove into my chest. I was ready to scream again, but as soon as it touched me, I realized it wasn't going to hurt me. It was whatever Geoffrey Noctofimus had stolen from me. It melted into me gently, and I felt all the colour in the world flooding back.

For a moment, there was silence.

Then all the other prisoners let out an angry roar and began yanking on their chains with obvious fury. Their handcuffs were not going to last much longer.

Behind me, I heard the cell door open. "Inspector Sands!" I cried, spinning around. "Thank God you—"

But it wasn't Inspector Sands who was standing there grinning at me.

"Well, well, well. Soak me in sack!" said Longface Lucky. "I told you as we'd find the young lady, didn't I? Dead or alive."

"It looks like she's the second possibility, and very soon going to be the first one, if you see what I mean," said Richard the Raker.

The two toshers were wearing clean white trousers and clean white shirts instead of the dirty jackets I had last seen them in, but I didn't have long to wonder at the change.

From all around the cell, I heard a series of sharp snaps that could only be one thing: chains breaking.

CHAPTER 21

*U*nder the circumstances, there wasn't much of a choice. I leapt through the door and slammed it behind me.

Richard the Raker grabbed my arm. I shook it off. "You guys know how to get out of here. I don't. I promise: until we get out of here, I'm sticking with you."

That satisfied Richard, but not Longface Lucky. "And as to after we gets out? Making any promises as to that?"

I bit my lip. I wasn't going to make any promises I couldn't keep. Unfortunately, my silence gave them all the information they needed. They each grabbed an arm and began dragging me down the corridor.

I didn't fight them. I figured I'd save my energy for when it counted.

"Where's Newfangled Troy?" I asked, as casually as I could ask anything while being dragged along a corridor.

Richard snorted angrily. "That lying laystall? We're well shot of him."

The toshers dragged me through a series of fluorescent-lit corridors with the same confidence they had displayed in the sewers. I wondered whether they just had a particularly good sense of direction, or if they had been here before.

The corridors grew more and more modern, with peeling white paint replacing stone walls, and faded linoleum replacing stone floors. We went through a set of swinging doors. This corridor didn't look any different to me, but Richard and Longface relaxed a little. "Nearly home free now," said Longface Lucky.

We turned another corner and found ourselves in the midst of the most bizarre creatures I had seen in ages.

Then I blinked, and I realized why they seemed so strange: they were completely normal. They were just ordinary people, with no horns, and with heads pointing the usual way on their necks. They were wearing clothes that hadn't been ripped to shreds by rats or soaked for hours in sewer water.

I had never felt more out of place in my life.

I was about to call to them for help when I saw what they were doing. They were sorting (non-glowing) mail into (non-magical-looking) carts. That meant they worked for the Royal Mail. I didn't know if that put them in league with the Saltpetre Men, but I couldn't risk it.

Fortunately, the magical alarm didn't seem to penetrate into this part of the facility. The workers ignored us as the toshers hurried me through the room, down a series of corridors, and out a door.

At long last, I was outside in daylight. In a moment, I would need to think about escaping, and then finding Lady Roslyn and my mom. But I gave myself a few seconds to take a deep breath and enjoy the sunlight on my face, and to gather my energy for my escape.

"Now then, missy," said Longface Lucky. "We've got us a buyer as we needs to see."

"A buyer? For what?" I asked.

They looked at me greedily, and I suddenly remembered I was a tosheroon.

OK. Energy gathered. Time for that escape.

I yanked my arms out from their hands and ran.

I made it a full two steps away before Richard the Raker tackled me. While he sat on me, Longface Lucky tied my wrists together.

He hailed a passing taxi. Richard heaved me up and threw me into the back of it.

"Sixty-eight Belsize Square," Longface told the driver.

"Ignore him!" I said. "These men are kidnapping me. Take us to the police."

"Ignore *her*," Longface said calmly. "This poor unfortunate lass ain't right in the head-like. She threw herself into the sewers, if you can believe such a thing. We're taking her back to the embrace of her family, which waits for her loving-like, at the address as what I gave you."

The driver looked at me in his rearview mirror. I could see his eyes taking in my filthy clothes. He sniffed, and I could imagine what I must have smelled like.

I realized why the toshers had dressed in white uniforms. They looked like orderlies from an insane asylum.

The driver nodded and focused his attention back on the road.

"I'm not crazy!" I yelled at him. "I'm not!"

Maybe that wasn't helping my case.

I struggled furiously with the ropes around my wrist, but they wouldn't budge.

"Don't you worry none," said Longface Lucky.

"The doctor as we're taking you to, he's going to fix you up, real special-like."

"You isn't going to have no complaints, never again, and that's the verulam," said Richard the Raker.

I still hadn't managed to get anywhere with the ropes around my wrists. Time to try a different approach. "Whoever this buyer is, I hope you're getting a good price for me."

"Oh, we'll be swimming in sausage. Don't you worry none," said Longface Lucky.

"Because if I was selling something valuable, I'd make sure I knew exactly what it was and what it could do, just so I didn't get cheated."

"Oh, we knows enough," said Richard the Raker. "We knows you keep turning up in significant places, and we know you wielded Bazalgette's Trowel, which means as your bloodline must be—"

Longface Lucky glared at him. "Phsh! Can't you see she's pumping you for knowledge? Shut your gob."

"Yes, Richard, listen to Lucky. He's obviously the brains of the operation."

Longface chuckled. "This little lady knows what's what."

I kept my eyes on Richard. "The problem is, the brain counts the money. And he what counts – I mean, he who counts the money gets to count it however he wants."

Longface wasn't chuckling any more. "I don't like as you're implying."

"You want me to shut *my* gob, too, is that it?"

"Right you is."

I nodded. "Hmm. Interesting. Well, Richard, Longface obviously doesn't want you to hear what I have to say, so I suppose I'd better shut up."

Richard's big eyes narrowed. "Now, just a minute, Longface Lucky. I don't see as how it's your leather if this girl wants to bring something to my attention."

I had to phrase what I said next very carefully. I couldn't lie outright, because for all I knew, I still had some river water in my lungs. "Gosh, Richard," I said. "Do *you* think Longface Lucky might have had some secret deal with Newfangled Troy?"

"That's preposterous!" Longface spluttered. "If you're saying I'd slice up a deal with that—"

"Oh, I'm not saying that! Not at all! But now that you mention it, if you *did* want to squeeze Richard out of his fair share, that would have been the perfect plan. Troy could pretend to steal Bazalgette's Trowel, you could let him get away, and then at some point, you could ditch Richard and meet up with Troy and split the cash."

"You shut up, young lady—"

"I notice you're not denying it," I interrupted.

"Hey!" Richard said. "Why isn't you denying it, Longface?"

"Fine!" Longface said. "I hereby—"

I couldn't afford to let him finish. "Yeah, Longface, why aren't you denying it?"

"I'm trying, but you keep—"

"You sure are taking your time with it."

"No, you're—"

"I don't think he's going to deny it," I told Richard. "I think he's going – What did you call it when Lady Roslyn did it? I think he's going around the glasshouse."

Richard was turning bright red with fury. "Is you pulling a glasshouse on me, Longface?"

Longface looked just as angry. "If you'd let me finish-like—"

"Yes, let him finish, Richard! Let him use that silver tongue of his to convince you of anything he wants! That's what he always does, isn't it?"

"It is!" Richard bellowed. "By God, it is!"

Richard jumped for Longface.

Which was exactly what I had been hoping would happen, but there was a flaw in my plan: starting a fistfight between two large, angry men probably would have been a better idea if I hadn't been sitting between them in the back of a taxi.

I tried to duck out of the way of their flying fists, but my hands were still tied behind my back, and I didn't exactly have a lot of room to manoeuvre. I'd say I took one punch for every three that either of them took.

Fortunately, they both got tired of hitting pretty quickly and moved on to choking each other. This didn't last long, either, because Longface Lucky's neck was as thick as his face was long, which is a pretty big advantage in a choking contest. Within moments, Richard's round face had turned bright purple, and his eyes were wobbling, and he had loosened his grip on Longface's neck. One hand still choking Richard, Longface swung open the door with his other. He shoved Richard onto the pavement.

Then he slammed the door and turned to me. "Our client was a-willing to pay more for you if you was alive, but I'm thinking the dosh ain't worth the dolours." He pulled a switchblade out of his pocket and flicked it open.

Before he could use it, the cab screeched to a stop. Longface and I both looked up in surprise as the driver hopped out of the front and swung open the rear door. "I believe we've arrived at your destination, sir."

Longface and I both looked out. We had pulled over in the middle of Blackfriars Bridge. "Is you daft?" Longface said. "This ain't where I'm getting out."

"Oh, I think it is, sir," the cab driver said, and for the first time, he bent down far enough that we could see his face. We both recognized him at once.

"Newfangled Troy?" shouted Longface Lucky. "What the dickens is—" Before he could finish the question, Troy placed one hand on Lucky's collar and one on his trousers and chucked him out of the cab. Lucky landed on a small piece of metal jutting out of the side of the bridge and dangled there above the water, futilely flailing.

All I could do was stare. "What are you – how did you – why—"

"Tell you what," Newfangled Troy said as he worked the knots around my wrists loose. "If you'll just trust me, I'll take you someplace where you can get some answers. Willing to put yourself in my hands?"

"Sure," I said, but only because this was the second time he had saved me, which proved he was trustworthy. My willingness to go with him had absolutely nothing to do with how cute he looked, especially now that he was all cleaned up and smelling even better.

Troy got back into the driver's seat and pulled away. I had so many questions to ask, I couldn't possibly choose, so I picked one pretty much at random.

"Are you old enough to get a licence?" I asked.

"You don't need a licence if you never get pulled over," he said.

"And what happened to your accent?" I asked.

Troy grinned and suddenly switched back to the thick, growly voice he had used when I met him: "What, you means, why ain't I talking all tosher-like?" Then he switched back to what I guessed was his London cabbie accent. "Sometimes you've got to hold down more than one job to make ends meet. And some jobs are easier to get if you talk the talk."

"But which one is your real voice?"

"They're both my real voice," he said. "I speak a lot of different languages." Then, in a pretty good imitation of my accent, he added, "I'm even learning American. How am I doing?"

"Sounds like you've been paying attention to me."

"Maybe I have." He laughed.

He turned off the main road, and we found ourselves on an underground road. Not a mysterious magical underground road – just an ordinary road running through a wide tunnel. Troy pulled up on the side of it, and we got out. He gestured to a little green shack tucked off to one side, next to a dingy pile of cardboard boxes. "A fine restaurant, exclusively for cab drivers and their honoured guests. After you."

I stepped through the door, followed by Troy. It was even dimmer inside than it was outside, and it took a moment for my eyes to adjust. When they did, I could see a small room, as narrow as a Tube car, with a tiny kitchen, a counter, and three tables squeezed in.

And in the back, behind one of the tables, sat Little Ben and Oaroboarus.

Troy nodded at them cheerfully, then held out his hand, palm up. "I believe you said something about cash on delivery?" he said.

CHAPTER 22

$\mathcal{I}$ stared at him. "They *paid* you to bring me to them?"

"I told you. Sometimes you've got to hold down more than one job to make ends meet."

Little Ben handed him a bulging envelope. Troy opened it up and rifled through the bundle of bills inside. "Looks right to me. A pleasure doing business with you." He turned towards the door.

"And now you're just leaving me with Little Ben? After you told me to put myself in your hands?" An unpleasant thought occurred to me. "Wait a minute. Was that like with Bazalgette's Trowel, where it was worth more if I gave it to you? Did you get more for me because I came willingly?"

Troy winked at me, which I did not consider a

satisfactory answer. Then he slipped out the door and was gone.

That lying laystall, I thought. I turned back to Little Ben. "What's to stop me from running out that door myself?"

"Wow, gosh, I guess nothing," Little Ben said. "Except maybe it would be kind of rude? Because I just paid Troy all the money I had to rescue you. Oh, but I saved enough to buy you a sandwich! And some tea!"

Oaroboarus rooted around in his pouch for a moment, then, one by one, threw a few cards onto the edge of the table.

"Why on earth would I want to do that?"

"Because the sandwiches here are pretty good?" Little Ben said.

"But…" I said. "But you're some kind of evil wizard or something."

There were a lot of different ways I might have imagined somebody would react to being called an evil wizard. But I wouldn't have expected the one Little Ben actually chose. He got a big smile on his face and started bouncing excitedly on his chair, like I had just told him it was his birthday. "Really? I am? That's pretty cool! I mean, I wouldn't like being evil, but I could reform. And then I'd still be a wizard!"

I WOULD NOT GET YOUR HOPES UP.

I SUSPECT SHE IS MERELY SPECULATING.

"I'm not speculating. I *know* you're evil. I sensed it!"

"Is that why you ran away the other time? You kind of hurt my feelings."

"I *hurt your feelings*?? I could sense your malice, deep in my bones."

Once again, he didn't react the way I expected. "Ooooh, cool! But wait. Why aren't you running away now? I should be just as evil as last time, right?"

He kind of had a point there. After the initial shock of seeing him and Oaroboarus had worn off, I wasn't feeling particularly frightened. He just seemed like an ordinary eleven-year-old boy. Or, at least, an ordinary eleven-year-old boy sitting next to an ordinary giant pig in a bathing suit.

Speaking of which. I turned to Oaroboarus. "What about you? You were snarling and baring your teeth at me!"

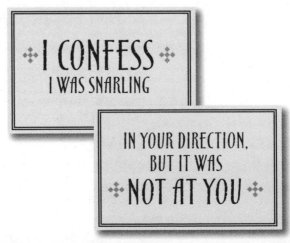

"If it wasn't at me, then who— Wait a minute. Oh, crap."

The "wait a minute" was when I remembered that Lady Roslyn had been standing right behind me. Which meant that Oaroboarus could have been growling at her instead of at me.

And the "Oh, crap" was when I remembered something even more important. Back when we were at the dusty old arcade, before we jumped down into the sewers, Lady Roslyn had made the top-hatted caretaker so terrified that he ran away, and all she had done was stand behind him and stare at him in a particular way. Had she done the same thing to me?

"You were snarling at Lady Roslyn? Why?"

SHE WAS LOOKING AT YOU ✢✢✢ WITH ✢✢✢ HER EYES

DISTURBINGLY WIDE, AND A MOST ALARMING EXPRESSION. IF YOU WILL FORGIVE ME BORROWING YOUR PHRASE,

I COULD SENSE HER MALICE DEEP IN MY BONES.

"You say that, but why should I believe some strange pig over a woman who has been helping me get my mom back— Oh, double crap."

Because as soon as I said it, I realized what had actually happened. Lady Roslyn had *me* sing open the sewer lid, which probably meant she couldn't do it herself. She had *me* guide her through the maze of conveyor belts to find where they were keeping Mom.

She hadn't helped me get my mom back. She had tricked *me* into helping *her* get Mom. But why did I have the magic abilities that made that possible? And if my powers were strong enough to create the drop of water on my own, why did Lady Roslyn even want Mom?

Richard the Raker had said something about my bloodline. Was I the daughter of some powerful sorceress? A powerful sorceress who didn't know the difference between pancakes and macaroni? Could she have had some magical mishap? Was she always like this, or did she accidentally drink from the Enchanted Chalice of Total Ditziness?

That didn't seem too likely. But if I was going to figure out something utterly unlikely, maybe there were worse people to talk to than a sewer-dwelling eleven-year-old and his giant pig. That didn't mean I was ready to trust them – but it meant that this time, I wasn't going to run away.

I sat down at the table.

Little Ben beamed. "Excellent!" he exclaimed.

MAY WE OFFER YOU
SOMETHING TO EAT?

I suddenly realized I hadn't eaten for ages, and I was starving. I looked up at the woman behind the counter. "I'll have a bacon sandw—" I began, and then I noticed Oaroboarus's horrified expression. I cleared my throat. "I mean, a tuna fish sandwich."

"And three teas, please," Little Ben added.

"Wait a minute," I said. "Last time we had tea, you did some kind of mind-control spell on me."

"I did?" he said. "I didn't mean to!"

"You must have," I told him. "Lady Roslyn said you did, and we were floating down the Tyburn, surrounded by magic, so she couldn't have lied, and …"

… and, I realized, she had been very, very careful in her phrasing. *It's entirely possible that he was giving you some wonderful, generous magical gift. But some people – less charitably inclined than I – might guess he was casting a spell on you.*

She had totally gone round the glasshouse on me. "Triple crap," I said. "You really were giving me some kind of magical gift?"

"That's what I was trying to do," Little Ben said. "I'm still trying to figure out how this magic stuff works, but I know that when you make tea in a certain way, it gives you a burst of inspiration. You looked pretty scared. I thought you could use some help."

"Is that why you paid Newfangled Troy all your money to rescue me? That seems awfully generous."

Little Ben blushed. "Well, to be honest, Newfangled Troy told me you were my only hope for finding out who I am. So it was a little selfish. But back in the sewers, I *was* just being nice! I didn't know you were my only hope then!"

The lady behind the counter handed over my sandwich and our teas. The whole restaurant was so small, she didn't even need to step out from behind the counter to do it.

I wanted some answers, plus I wanted a few minutes to wolf down the first food I'd had in who knows how long. So I told Little Ben, "Start at the beginning. Tell me everything."

CHAPTER 23

"A couple of months ago," Little Ben said, "I woke up in that room in the sewers where you found me. I couldn't remember who I was or how I got there, or anything else. But I was holding a note in my hands. Here."

Little Ben fished around in his pockets and pulled out a well-worn piece of paper. He handed it to me, and I stopped stuffing my face long enough to read it:

Dear Little Ben,
    I know this will seem alarming to you, but fear not. In time, it will all make sense.
    Sincerely,
    Benjamin

"While I was trying to figure out what that meant," Little Ben continued, "Oaroboarus came in. He looked pretty surprised to see me."

I EXPECTED TO SEE BENJAMIN, THE OLD MAN WHO PRINTED MY CARDS FOR ME

I HAD BEEN VISITING THAT ROOM FOR TWO DECADES

AND THERE HAD NEVER BEEN A CHILD THERE

Little Ben nodded. "I guessed that maybe Benjamin was my father, and he kept me hidden for some reason, maybe? Or maybe I was away and when I came back, there was a curse on me that robbed me of my memory, and so he went off on a quest to get my memory back? Anyway, now you're here, and you can explain everything to me!"

By now, I had swallowed my entire sandwich, and I was ready to talk again. But I didn't know what to say. "Wow. Um. I don't know why Troy told you that. I've got no idea who you are."

Little Ben's face fell. Oaroboarus gave me a stern look, and I knew exactly what it meant, since I'd often gotten it from my grandmother and various aunts. It meant, *You can do better than that.* I couldn't help feeling guilty, so I searched my memory. "All I know is what Lady Roslyn told me. She said she knew a lot about you. And that you didn't always take the form of a young boy. Maybe that would explain why Oaroboarus never saw you before?"

"Ooooh, I can shape-shift? Cool! I'm going to try it right now! Abracadabra – form of a mighty eagle!" He scrunched up his face in an expression of intense concentration, but nothing happened. He still looked like an eleven-year-old boy. "Awww. I guess not."

"Look, I'd really like to help you, and I appreciate the whole paying-to-have-me rescued thing, plus this was a great sandwich. But I kind of have my own missing parent to figure out."

"Hey! Maybe that's what Troy meant! He didn't say you knew who I was. He said you were the key to my figuring it out. Maybe that means I'm supposed to help you, and I'll find my answers along the way." He must have noticed my sceptical look, because he added, "I know lots of stuff that might be useful. You saw all those filing cabinets in the print room? I've been searching through them ever since I woke up, looking for clues. I haven't found anything about me yet, but there's a ton of stuff about magic, and the history of the underground rivers. And it turns out I can remember everything I read perfectly – maybe because my memory was blank to start off with, so there's plenty of room. Tell me what you need to do. Maybe I'll know something about it!"

Should I trust him? Since I was sitting with a giant pig, presumably there was enough magic around that something would have exploded if Little Ben had been lying. He must have genuinely believed everything he told me. But by the same principle, Lady Roslyn must have genuinely believed that he didn't always appear in the form of an eleven-year-old. So what were the possibilities? Could the old man whom Oaroboarus had known have transformed into the shape of a child for a nefarious purpose, and then somehow forgotten he had done it? Or could the old man have summoned a child-shaped demon and lost control of it, and then the demon had eaten him too quickly, resulting in some kind of indigestion-related amnesia?

I thought back to when I had come to Little Ben's underground room, shivering and wet. He had offered me a blanket, and the expression on his face had been one of genuine concern and sympathy. It wasn't a lot to go on, but it was something I had seen with my own eyes.

And anyway, what alternatives did I have at the moment? I decided I'd take a chance on Little Ben. I filled him in on everything that had happened.

When I was done, he shook his head. "One thing I can tell you is, Lady Roslyn wasn't very fair to the other side. The anarchists, she called them? I think my dad was one. I found a lot of articles and pamphlets and posters in his files about how everybody should have access to the power of the rivers. Only, the people who wrote those pamphlets didn't call themselves anarchists. They called themselves Egalitarians. And they never said anything about the Inheritors of Order. They called people who disagreed with them the Elitists, and the Elitists *definitely* sounded like the bad guys."

"But the anarchists – I mean, the Egalitarians – you guys started World War One."

"Hey, don't blame me!" Little Ben said. "I might not remember much, but I'm pretty sure I wasn't even born then! But I admit, all those pamphlets I read just showed one side of the story. Maybe there's goodies and baddies on both teams."

IT WAS THE
ELITISTS
WHO STARTED

THE GREAT FIRE
OF LONDON.

"Lady Roslyn said the Egalitarians did that," I said, but then stopped myself. "No, I guess she didn't. She phrased it pretty carefully so I jumped to the wrong conclusion … again. Anyway, whoever did it, why would somebody want to burn down the whole city?"

Oaroboarus shrugged and handed me a card with a single word on it.

"I don't care which side is right. I just want to get my mom back. How are we going to do that?"

"Wow. I have no idea. I don't think a cup of tea is going to be enough inspiration for this one. We better put on our thinking caps."

Oaroboarus stuck his snout into a large carpet-bag that was sitting on the chair next to him and pulled out three silk top hats. He tossed one to Little Ben and one to me, and then flipped the last one onto his own head.

"Top hats?" I asked.

"One of the things I found in the filing cabinet was a collection of hats, all labelled with the year they came from. I couldn't figure out what hats had to do with magic. So I tried arranging them by age, and I noticed they got shorter and shorter as time went on. Now, one thing I already knew was, there's some kind of connection between the river water and inspiration."

I nodded. "Which is why tea gives you inspiration. Or mixing hot and cold water in the shower – Lady Roslyn mentioned that."

"Exactly. So I started thinking, maybe inspiration comes out through the top of your head? And maybe hats stopped it from floating away? And maybe the bigger the hat, the more inspiration it could store?"

I stared at him. "I admit, I'm sitting here drinking tea with a giant pig and an amnesiac eleven-year-old I met in the sewer, so I'm not really in a position to say this, but doesn't that sound crazy to you?"

"It doesn't matter if people call a new idea crazy. What matters is what the evidence says."

"But you said hats have been getting smaller over time. Isn't that evidence that bigger hats aren't better?"

Little Ben shook his head. "Something the Egalitarian pamphlets kept talking about was, the Elitists work really hard to keep magic away from ordinary people. You remember how Lady Roslyn told you that if you put the milk in first, then the tea, it neutralizes the magic? Well, if you go to a poor home, guess which order they'll do it in? And she told you that if you put the tea in first, then the milk, it makes the magic more powerful? Well, guess how aristocrats make tea?"

"What does that have to do with hats?" I asked.

"It's the same thing! Look at how people dress at the Ascot races versus a football match— In fact, hold on, I might even have the photos here…"

He rifled around in the carpet-bag and pulled out two photographs. One showed a bunch of extremely well-dressed men and women watching a horse race, sipping champagne. Every one of them was wearing a huge, ornate hat. The other photo was a soccer game (or football match, as I guess I was supposed to call it). Everybody's head was completely bare.

"You see?" Little Ben said. "Somehow, over a couple of centuries, ordinary people have gone from wearing big hats to leaving their heads uncovered, while rich people haven't. Doesn't that prove something?"

"Police officers still wear hats," I said. "I don't know many police officers with mansions."

"Oooh, good point!" Little Ben said. He thought about it for a minute. "But that just proves that working-class people can get fully inspired if the Elitists need them to keep order."

"But if *that's* true," I said, "then the more important person you were protecting, the bigger hat you'd get, and ..." A thought occurred to me. "... and that's why the guards at Buckingham Palace have the tallest hats ever. OK. Score one for the amnesiac with the giant pig." I picked up the top hat and plopped it on my head.

We all sat there, concentrating. Gradually, I could feel an idea beginning to stir. Something about the Great Fire? I waited but nothing else came.

I remembered something Aunt Mel used to say: *Genius is one per cent inspiration, ninety-nine per cent perspiration.* Maybe the tea could give me the initial inspiration, and the hat could help me hold on to it – but after that, I'd have to work the idea out myself. "Lady Roslyn told me that the Great Fire started because somebody mixed hot and cold water," I said, figuring it out as I spoke. "When I mixed hot and cold water, it made that powerful drop of water. Maybe that's why the Elitists did it. They didn't *mean* to start a Great Fire; they just wanted to make a powerful drop to take control of the river."

"That makes sense," Little Ben said.

"And maybe they didn't know the Great Fire was even a possibility. But Lady Roslyn does, so she wouldn't do whatever they did, would she? I mean, she wouldn't risk burning the whole city down, would she?"

"You know her better than I do," Little Ben said. "Does she seem like a reasonable person?"

Gulp. "We've got to stop her. But how? The Great Fire started in a baker's oven. If she's trying to do the same thing, maybe she'd try to start in the same place. She said the oven was at... Um..."

Fortunately, Little Ben knew the answer. "It was on Pudding Lane," he said, jumping to his feet. "And I think we'd better get going."

CHAPTER 24

*N*ear Pudding Lane, in a wide courtyard set off by wooden bollards, there was a tall stone monument to the Great Fire. It was called the Monument, and it was on Monument Street. I guess sometimes, cities just kind of give up on naming things.

Little Ben, Oaroboarus, and I stood there for a moment reading the plaque on the side of the Monument. "It doesn't say anything about how to stop the Great Fire from happening again," Little Ben said.

"Here's something weird," I said. "It says the Monument is two hundred two feet tall, because it's two hundred two feet from where the fire began. Which stops making sense as soon as you think about it. If you lay the Monument on its side, it'll stretch to the actual spot the fire started, but who's going to lay it on its side? Why not just put the Monument on the actual spot to begin with?"

"I don't know," Little Ben said. "But one thing I've learned from my research. Ninety per cent of British life makes total sense. The other ten per cent seems absolutely bonkers … *if* you don't know about the secret rivers. So if you're trying to find magic, it's that ten per cent you have to pay attention to."

We stepped through the door at the base of the Monument into a small, dim entrance hall. There was a ticket seller sitting there. He took one look at Oaroboarus and shook his head. "No pets."

I pointed to my ears and tried to look confused. Then I turned to Oaroboarus. "What's that? What did he say?" I asked.

Oaroboarus caught on immediately.

HE SAID
NO PETS ALLOWED!

I turned back to the ticket seller. "You allow service animals, don't you?"

"That usually means dogs."

"What did he say?" I asked Oaroboarus.

HE SAID
THAT USUALLY
MEANS DOGS!

The ticket seller looked at Oaroboarus, then looked at me, then shrugged. "Two pounds for each human under the age of sixteen. No charge for service pigs."

When we had climbed out of earshot, I gave Oaroboarus a little salute. "Nicely done. Great thinking on your feet. But how did you have exactly the right cards to repeat what he said?"

I HAVE CARDS
FOR EVERY
OCCASION.

"*Every* occasion? What if the Queen of England spilled peanut butter on your pet electric eel?"

THAT WOULD BE IMPOSSIBLE.

I HAVE NO PETS.

ELECTRIC OR OTHERWISE

"Then you *don't* have cards for every occasion!"

Oaroboarus squinted at me stubbornly and rooted around in his card box. I was sure he was just bluffing, but no:

FEAR NOT, YOUR MAJESTY.

LITTLE SHOCKY-HEAD

DOES **NOT** HAVE A NUT ALLERGY.

"Wow," I said. "You're *good*."

Oaroboarus grunted modestly. We kept climbing.

And climbing.

And climbing.

"Two hundred two feet seemed like a lot less when we were at the bottom," I said.

I had never really thought much about what kind of spiral staircases I prefer, but as we got higher and higher, I started thinking about it more and more. Some spiral staircases have walls on both sides. Those, I decided, are the right kind. In other spiral staircases, there's no wall on one side, just a handrail, so you can see all the way down the stairwell, and it gets more and more dizzying as you get higher and higher. That's the wrong kind of spiral staircase.

The Monument? Definitely the wrong kind.

And then we were at the top. We stepped out into the sunlight of the viewing platform.

The view from the top was the highest view yet, but since I wasn't looking straight down a big spiral, it wasn't anywhere near as dizzying.

There was a metal railing all around the edge of the platform. In fact, the metal railing stretched all the way above our heads, then curved back to form a metal roof. It was like we were standing inside a birdcage.

"That's weird, too, don't you think?" I asked Little

Ben. "I get why there's a fence in front of us. You don't want people falling off the edge. But why is there a fence *above our heads*? What, are we going to fall up?"

"Maybe they're worried people will climb the fence and jump off?"

"Then make the fence tall or put pointy bits on the top, or both. But why put a huge fence where the ceiling would be? To keep people from flying away?"

I looked around, hoping to find more of that crazy ten per cent. All I saw on the walls was ancient graffiti – somebody calling themselves TIID had apparently been here in 1792, and to carve their initials and the date into the wall, they must have had a chisel and a hammer with them.

The floor was more interesting. Built into it was a small drain, ending in an iron grate. A few days ago, I wouldn't have paid much attention to drainage. But after the past twenty-four hours…

I pointed at the drain. "Look at this. All drains connect to the sewers eventually, right? So this is like an outlet in a house – it's a connection to the power source. But … how do we switch it on?" I felt an idea tickling the back of my mind, but it kept slipping out of my grasp.

Oaroboarus stuck his snout into Little Ben's carpetbag, pulled out a top hat, and handed it to me.

I put it on my head, and I could feel the thought that kept slipping out of my head bounce right back. It was a memory.

I had always gotten along better with Dad than with Mom, but there was one thing about him that drove me crazy: he'd rather do something badly himself than pay somebody else to do it well. Usually, I could live with that. When he tried to fix our windows and just made them draftier, I could put on a sweater. When he tried to fix a fuse and ended up plunging the whole house into darkness, I could read with a flashlight. But when he messed up the plumbing, the consequences were absolutely disgusting.

Today, after all I had been through underground, Dad's screw-ups seemed pretty mild in retrospect. But when I was nine and he messed up our sink so that the smell of sewage wafted up from it, I was horrified. In fact, that's what had inspired me to learn some plumbing basics myself, so that I could fix his mistakes.

Anyway, here's the key thing I remembered: our sink always smelled worst right after we had used it. As the water went down the drain and into the sewage deep below, it stirred up the odours, sending them floating back up.

So there was my hat-given inspiration. Now I just needed to put in a little work. "Maybe if we pour water down this drain," I said, "it will stir up the sewer down below, and the magic will come floating up."

Little Ben shook his head. "If it were that simple, then it would happen every time it rained. And it rains a lot. Magic is usually better hidden than that."

I thought some more. "I bet we need river water."

"Oooh! Good idea. But I didn't bring any."

"Me neither. A few hours ago, I could have just wrung out my hair and my clothes, but now I've dried out completely."

I DRINK NOTHING BUT
ENCHANTED
RIVER WATER.

IF YOU WOULD KINDLY
AVERT YOUR EYES...

"Avert my eyes from what?" I asked.

Beneath his thick bristles, Oaroboarus blushed, and I realized what he was getting at. "Oh!" I said. "You mean... Sure, no problem."

Little Ben and I looked up at the sky. There was a rustling noise, which I assume was Oaroboarus lowering his bathing suit. Then there was the sound of flowing water, which I pretended not to notice. I whistled casually.

When the water sound had stopped and I had heard the rustling of cloth again, I figured it was safe to look. Oaroboarus was back in his suit, and a thin yellow stream was wending its way down the drainage channel.

The last drops vanished, and nothing happened. "Oh, well," I said. "It was worth a—"

And then I heard a rattling. I looked down and spotted a discarded soda bottle rolling along the ground. *Odd,* I thought. *Why would it be rolling, unless—*

Oh, boy. "The Monument is tilting!" I cried. The bottle bumped into the railing, slipped between the rails, and went plummeting twenty storeys down to the street below.

And as the tower kept tilting, I felt gravity pulling me along, too. I tried to lean back, but the tilt was too strong, and I lunged forwards. I managed to keep upright for the first few steps, and then I crashed into the wire railing. Little Ben plunged into it next to me. Oaroboarus held out a little longer – I guess because he had two extra legs and a lower centre of gravity – but as the Monument tilted farther and farther, he slammed into the fence, too. His massive bulk shook the railing so furiously, I worried it would break open.

But it held.

And the tower kept tilting, faster and faster, until it was no longer tilting but *falling*, and the square below was rushing up towards us, and buildings shot by, and we were just about to hit the ground –

– but the Monument slammed into the wooden bollards on the ground, and the bollards sank down into the courtyard, somehow absorbing the full force of the tumbling stone tower. It came to a sudden stop.

Now, this next bit is a little confusing, so you'll have to work with me for a minute. Look up at the ceiling of the room you're in, and imagine that the building suddenly fell over on its side. That ceiling would now be the wall. And if the building fell fast enough, you'd get thrown straight into the ceiling-that-was-now-a-wall.

And if that building were the Monument, and the ceiling were made out of birdcage wire, you'd get thrown straight into it, and you'd suddenly understand why the balcony has a ceiling in the first place. It's to catch people who get thrown forwards when the Monument topples over.

Which is exactly what happened to me, Little Ben, and Oaroboarus.

The wire cage stretched out, slowly bringing us to a stop, and I was just beginning to feel like I'd come through this without any injuries, when it snapped back like an overextended trampoline, and we all crashed into the stone floor.

But of course, the stone floor was now an upright stone wall, so we slid right down it and landed on the wire railing of the wall that was the new floor. (Confused? Hey, try living through it.)

The whole thing had shaken a single card out of Oaroboarus's box. It fluttered down and landed in my lap.

Ouch.

"Tell me about it," I said. But then I noticed something that took my mind off my bruises. (OK, *mostly* took my mind off *most* of my bruises.)

When the Monument had been standing upright like a monument is supposed to, there had been a metal statue of a flame on the very top of the wire cage, above our heads. Now that the Monument was lying on its side, that flame touched the plaque that marked the actual spot where the fire had begun.

A spark leapt out of the plaque and onto the metal flame. For an instant, the metal erupted into real fire. As it turned back to metal, the spark flowed out into the wire fence around us, and then all the way down through the Monument, right to the ground where the column had stood before it fell over. And as the spark sank down into the earth, the ground opened, revealing a massive hole.

"I think we have to get into that hole," I said.

If the monument had been standing upright, we would have just walked down the staircase. But when you lay a spiral staircase on its side, it turns into a bunch of curvy stone walls.

I climbed carefully over the first one, followed by Little Ben, and as I was making my way over the second, a fat comet barely cleared the space above my head.

It was Oaroboarus, leaping several sets of steps at once. He made it halfway down the staircase (or, I guess, the staircase-themed obstacle course) before he stopped and looked back, as if it had only just occurred to him that humans couldn't keep up.

Then he thundered back to where we were and bent his legs. Little Ben climbed up onto his back immediately, but I hesitated. Somehow, it seemed like kind of an insult to Oaroboarus's dignity. "Is that – do you mind? I mean—"

I ASSURE YOU:
IT WOULD BE AN HONOUR.

I climbed up behind Little Ben. And with an effortless flick of his mighty legs, Oaroboarus was off, bounding over the little stone walls like a sprinter gliding over hurdles. Giant boars don't come with handles, so I had to cling to his back. His bristles pressed into my face a little uncomfortably, and I nearly bounced off every time he crashed to the ground – but it was still one of the most comfortable ways I had travelled lately. It certainly beat being swept along a sewer or carried by rats.

We reached the entry room at the (former) base of the tower. The ticket seller was sprawled out on a (former) wall. He blinked at us with a dazed look and mumbled, "Twice in one day?"

"What do you mean?" I asked him, but before he could answer, Oaroboarus leapt up through the door, which was now on the ceiling.

And then we fell into the hole under the Monument.

CHAPTER 25

*A*nd we fell and fell and fell.

We must have dropped for a good twenty feet, and when we finally hit the ground, I could feel the force of our landing ripple through the thick layer of fat on Oaroboarus's back. It was nearly enough to throw me off, but I clung tightly until everything settled down.

Cautiously, I lifted my head.

We were in a wide, deep hole. The walls were mostly black earth, but running around them a few inches above our heads was a line of red clay. Something about that line looked familiar, but I couldn't quite put my finger on what.

Sunk into the dirt floor was a big, old-looking

stone pedestal. There were two metal rods sticking out of the top, as though they once had held something up in the air. Whatever they had held was now gone. That, plus what the ticket seller had said about "twice in one day", could only mean one thing.

"Lady Roslyn got here first," I said.

"Looks like it," Little Ben said. "But what did she take?"

I looked more closely at the pedestal and noticed words carved into the base. They were faded and dirty and easy to overlook, but I could still make out the words: FALCEM ENIM IGNUM.

"That means 'fire hook' in Latin," Little Ben said. Then he stopped and grinned. "Ooooh! Cool! I know Latin! Is that something most kids know?"

"No, it's pretty impressive," I said. "But shouldn't you have forgotten Latin along with everything else?"

Little Ben thought about it. "When I got amnesia, I must have forgotten all the facts I knew, but not the skills. They're probably stored in different parts of the brain. After all, I can still walk and feed myself and speak English – I'm not like a newborn baby or anything."

"Good," I said. "I've dealt with enough poop for one day. OK, so this was a fire hook. What's a fire hook?"

"I read about that in my dad's files. Back in 1666,

there wasn't any way to put out a big fire. The best you could do was to pull down the buildings nearby before they caught fire, so it wouldn't spread."

I thought about it. "Lady Roslyn showed me a rune that was a picture of a clay pot. Clay pots control water, so that rune gives people power over the magic from the rivers. Maybe fire hooks give people control over magic relating to fire. And given how much trouble they took with it, the one stored here must have been a particularly important one."

Little Ben looked worried. "In that case, if Lady Roslyn has it—"

Before he could finish, Oaroboarus let out a frantic snort and started throwing a shower of cards at my feet.

IF YOU WILL PARDON THE INTERRUPTION,

I ADVISE YOU TO CEASE CONVERSATION AS SOON AS POSSIBLE

AND TO DIRECT YOUR GAZE UPWARDS.

NOW!

I looked up and gasped. Over our heads, the top of the hole was beginning to close up. The Monument was slowly rising back into place.

Little Ben leapt onto Oaroboarus's back, and I jumped on behind him. With a mighty bound, Oaroboarus shot upwards.

He almost made it. His hooves touched the top edge of the hole and he scrabbled frantically, but with our weight on his back, he couldn't pull himself up. He plummeted back down, hitting the ground with a loud THUMP.

He paused, caught his breath, bent his legs, and was about to spring up once more –

– when something started coming out of the walls. Right at the level where the circle of red clay ran around the room, lumps pushed forwards out of the dirt. They resolved themselves into faces, then heads. Grey heads, made out of London clay, with red bands running around them at eye level.

The heads of Saltpetre Men.

Dozens of them.

Lower down on the wall, other lumps solidified into hands, pushing outwards.

The hands broke through, and we were surrounded. The Saltpetre Men lumbered towards us.

Oaroboarus sprang up, up, up, and this time, he

was high enough to grab the top of the pit with his front hooves. He began to scramble up.

And I began to slip down.

"Help!" I yelled. Little Ben turned around, saw what was happening, and grabbed my wrist just as I slid off. Oaroboarus made it up and over the edge of the pit, and for a moment, I thought I was home free.

That's when a clammy, crumbling hand grabbed my ankle.

I kicked frantically, but the Saltpetre Man wouldn't loosen his grip, and all I accomplished was to slip out of Little Ben's grasp completely –

– but I didn't fall far, because Oaroboarus spun around and snuffled up my hand into his massive snout. I could feel the sharp edge of his long row of teeth, but he had a surprisingly delicate touch, and his teeth held me there without piercing my skin.

Oaroboarus tugged on one side, and a Saltpetre Man tugged on the other, and I hung there, half in and half out of the hole, every joint in my body stretching like it was going to pop.

Then more Saltpetre Men grabbed my feet, and I started inching downwards.

All the while, the Monument had been slowly rising up into its usual place. By now, there was only the narrowest gap left. Oaroboarus already had to duck to hold on to me. But the base of the Monument was getting lower and lower, forcing his snout farther and farther down.

The Saltpetre Men kept pulling. I kept inching towards them.

Oaroboarus tossed his head, and somehow, without letting my wrist slip out of his gentle teeth, he speared my sleeve with his tusks. But it wasn't enough. There were too many Saltpetre Men, and they were going to pull me down, and that stupid stubborn pig wasn't going to let go until his snout was crushed under a giant stone monument.

"Let go," I said.

He ignored me.

I felt a sharp pain in my shoulders, as if my arms were coming out of their sockets.

"You're not helping either of us!" I yelled. "They're going to pull me apart!"

"Let her go, you dummy!" Little Ben yelled. I could see the Monument's stone base pushing deeper and deeper into Oaroboarus's snout. He must have been in as much pain as I was, but still he refused to let go. If we waited any longer, his mouth and my limbs were going to shatter.

With a desperate, yanking twist, I managed to

pull my arm out of his mouth. The sleeve ripped off my shirt, and I fell into the darkness and the clammy, waiting hands.

CHAPTER 26

In the faint remaining light, I could make out a seething mass of misshapen figures. The ones that weren't already holding my legs grabbed on to my arms and hoisted me up between them. I struggled and fought back. They didn't seem to notice.

I wondered what they thought they were going to do with me. The only human-accessible way out had just been sealed by the Monument.

Then the Saltpetre Men began to flow back into the dirt wall.

"You're not going to try and take me through—" I started, and then I had to stop, because they had just carried me into the wall, and the dirt was rushing into my mouth. I slammed it shut before I could choke.

When I tried to breathe through my nose, I inhaled nothing but dirt.

I held my breath.

We were going somewhere – I could feel the clammy earth flowing across my skin – but I had no idea where, or how long it would take us to get there. I held my breath as long as I could, and then I held it longer. My eyes were closed, but I saw pink and red flashes. My lungs spasmed in my chest, like they had decided if I wasn't going to use them, they were darn well going to get some exercise on their own. All I wanted to do was to open my mouth and take a huge breath, but I couldn't, I couldn't, because there was only dirt there, and now my lungs had stopped spasming and started thrashing, and my eardrums felt like they were going to burst, although I didn't know whether it was from the breath inside pushing outwards, or the dirt outside pushing inwards, and the red and pink flashes were beginning to fade away, which was even scarier than seeing them, and I had to, I had to open my mouth and inhale whatever was there, so I tried to do it, but I couldn't because the sheer weight of the earth was holding my mouth shut and oh, God, I was going to die and—

CHAPTER 27

$\mathcal{A}$nd the weight lifted and my mouth flew open, and I sucked in a lifetime's worth of air. It was stale and damp, but it tasted as sweet as farm air to me. I was so busy breathing, I took a dozen breaths before I realized I could open my eyes, too.

I was in another dirt-walled room, but this one was smaller, with a low roof. I was surrounded by masses of Saltpetre Men, and one of them must have been holding a flashlight – I could see the beam bending as it filtered through a dozen misshapen bodies.

Then, one by one, the creatures melted back into the wall. Each one that vanished left the flashlight beam a little less fragmented, until it was a strong, steady beam, held by a single Saltpetre Man.

"Hello, Hyassinth," Inspector Sands said. He was leaning against a closed door that looked like the only exit. The flashlight was tucked under his arm as he flipped through a folder full of papers.

By then, I had finished gasping and choking, but I was still too angry to speak. Finally, I got out the words, "They almost killed me."

"Yess, my men sseem to have forgotten that humanss have lungss. My apologiess."

He said it so casually, without even looking up from his papers, that it only made me angrier. "Your *apologies*? That's the second time you've almost gotten me killed. I want to speak to your supervisor."

He finally looked up, and I thought I saw something like amusement glitter in his mica eyes. "My sssssupervisssssor?" he said, drawing out the word as though he found it delicious. "Truly, you do not wissh to sspeak with my sssssupervisssssor. If szhe had had her way, my men would have taken you under the dirt and left you there."

"Why would she want me dead?"

"You desstroy a Royal Mail offiss. You break out of a magical holding fassility, freeing dozhenss of highly dangerouss beingss in the procsess. Then King Charless'ss Fire Hook dissappearss, and when my men arrive at the sscene, they disscover you, and you attempt to flee.

You musst admit, it'ss all a bit susspisciouss."

"But the hook was already gone when I got there."

"Indeed. My men do not move with great sspeed. The Monument wass opened for the firsst time sseveral hourss ago; it hass taken uss thiss long to resspond. I believe that whoever took the Fire Hook wass long gone by the time we arrived. When my ssupervissor ordered me to kill you, I pointed thiss out to her, and zshe grudgingly permitted me to bring you in alive."

"Oh. Well. Then, thank you." Embarrassed, I lowered my eyes, and for the first time, I noticed the words written on the folder he was holding: *Hayward, Hyacinth.* "Is that my police file?"

"Your medical recordss. I ssee you have not been vaccsinated againsst ssmallpoxx." He pulled a needle out of the folder.

"And why does that – ow!" I had forgotten how much faster he could move than the other Saltpetre Men – he had the needle in my arm before I could finish the question. And before I could say anything else, he pulled out a spray bottle and spritzed me in the face with something disgusting. "Eww! What was that?"

"Conssentrated sspore of the ground beetle, which iss the only creatzhure that eatss fleass. There iss no vaccsine for the bubonic plague. The mosst one can do iss frighten away the fleass that carry it."

"Wait, the *plague*? Where are we?"

Instead of answering, he pulled an ancient-looking key out of his pocket and unlocked the door. Then he went through it. I didn't know what else to do, so I followed him.

He led me into a roughly dug room, just tall enough for us to stand upright under a dirt ceiling held up by a scattering of wood planks. He shined his flashlight all around, and everywhere it touched, the light picked out splintered shapes that gleamed white, then vanished into blackness as the beam passed on.

"Those white things," I said. "Are they…"

"Boness," he answered. "When the Black Death sstruck London, the corpssess piled up sso fasst that the living could not bury the dead. Insstead, they szhoveled them into plague pitss like thiss one, buried asz deep asz they could dig."

"But that was hundreds of years ago. Surely I wouldn't still need a vaccine."

"We are twenty feet below the ground. There iss no ssunszhine and little oxzygen. Your kind cannot lasst long in thesze conditionss – but other thingss can ssurvive for ssenturiess. Come, I have ssomething to sshow you, and it iss besst if we finissh while there iss sstill oxzygen for you."

He glided ahead. I tried to follow and stumbled

over a mound of something, sending hard white balls rolling in all directions: skulls.

As I hurried after him, I wondered why he was walking so much more smoothly than I was. Then I looked down at his feet. They were gliding *through* the piles of dirt and bone, seamlessly merging in and out of the wavy ground. I remembered how awkwardly he had walked on a linoleum floor, and I couldn't help thinking of a movie I had seen about penguins. On land, they waddled awkwardly. Underwater, they were astonishingly agile.

Watching Inspector Sands move through the dirt, I knew I was seeing him in his element.

He led me past endless piles of skulls. "You ssee here the remainss of a thoussand or sso of your kind. Thesze are the fruitss of a ssingle day of the Black Death. A ssingle day'ss harvesst, in only one of numerouss pitss. But thiss pit iss sspeczial."

He knelt down and began picking through a pile of bones. "Thiss pit iss the *firsst*. Thosze buried here were the firsst oness to fall ill. And that iss becausse they were the oness who created the plague."

"Somebody *created* it? Who would do that?"

Inspector Sands found what he was looking for: a golden necklace inside an ancient ribcage. He picked it up and held it up to his flashlight so that

I could see the charm hanging from it.

It was the zombie bunny rabbit. The upside-down Sherlock Holmes. The ancient rune of the urn.

"These people – they belonged to the Inheritors of Order? Lady Roslyn's ancestors? But *why?*"

"The plague wass a magical weapon. A cursse, you might call it. It wass ssupposed to be carefully targeted againsst the enemiess of the Inheritorss. But your kind can never control thesze thingss asz well asz you exzpect."

I stared at the charm. It was smudged, but other than that, it could have been the same one Lady Roslyn wore. "I guess Little Ben's dad is on the right side," I said.

Inspector Sands shook his head. "There iss no right sside. There are only right actionss. I szhall take you one level up."

He held out his hand, and I took it. Then he touched the ceiling with his other hand. "I advizhe you to hold your breath," he said.

After my recent experience, when a Saltpetre Man told me to hold my breath, I was going to listen. I held my breath.

Inspector Sands jumped up, straight through the rock ceiling. I had a moment to close my eyes, and then I was yanked along with him.

It turns out that being pulled through solid rock is even weirder than being pulled through dirt. It was like every inch of my body was being rubbed endlessly by one of Aunt Mel's loofahs. I was sorry she wasn't there with me – she was really into exfoliation.

Fortunately, this trip was much shorter. In a few seconds, we emerged out of the rock into a small tunnel, low enough that Inspector Sands had to stoop down. "Two hundred and fifty yearss after the Black Death, a man named Guy Fawkess and hiss friendss dug thiss passage. Their plan wass to tunnel under the Housse of Lordss and plant enough gunpowder to desstroy the building, murdering the hundresss of people insside, including the king and all the arisstocraczy of the natzion. Asz it happened, they found an eassier way to get under the Housse of Lordss, and they abandoned thiss tunnel ... but not before carving thiss."

He shined his light against the wall, and I could see a shape carved in the stone:

"What's that?" I asked.
"The ssymbol of the Egalitarianss."

I refused to believe him. If one side created the Black Plague, and the other had tried to murder the entire Parliament, who was I supposed to root for?

Then I realized what the shape was. It was a tall hat. I thought of the collection of hats Little Ben had found in his dad's files, and the conclusion it had led him to: if everybody had tall hats, everybody would have equal access to magical inspiration.

Tall hats as a symbol of magical equality. It made a disturbing amount of sense. "So *everybody* is evil? Great. I'm glad they gave you a position of authority. You must be a real inspirational leader."

Instead of answering, Inspector Sands held up a finger and whispered, "Lissten."

In the silence, I could hear a faint rustling noise. Rats? Fleas?

Inspector Sands pointed his flashlight at a distant wall, where I could see something moist glistening. He led me closer to it, and I saw that it was simply a stream of water, trickling down from a crack on the ceiling and vanishing into the dirt below.

"Thiss iss new. There wass no stream here yessterday. That drop of water you sset loosse hass been caussing havoc all along the ssecret riverss. Thiss tunnel here, the plague pit below – they call to the Tyburn, and the sspark you created hass given the Tyburn the power to answwer. If we cannot recover that losst drop, thiss trickle on the wall will become a torrent, and the dirt will waszh away, and the plague pit will be open to the air. And the plague that hass sstayed buried for ssenturiess will sspill out."

"And it will be my fault," I said. I felt so awful that I couldn't say anything else.

"No," Inspector Sands said. "That iss my point … Do you know how the Great Fire sstarted?"

"Oaroboarus told me the Inheritors of Order started it."

"Yess. They did not intend to sstart the Fire – they ssimply wanted to generate the power to kill their enemiess. Do you know what the Fire did? It killed only ten humanss – but millionss of ratss and fleass, and that brought an end to the Black Death, and that ssaved hundredss of thoussandss of livess. Sssssso. They tried to do ssomething evil, which caussed an entirely different catasstrophe, which ssomehow ended up ssaving livess. How do you judgze them?"

"They were trying to kill people," I said. "They don't get credit for anything good that came out of it."

"Jusst sso. And *you* don't get the blame for conssequencess you could not foressee. You were merely trying to wassh your handss. What makess you good or evil are the actionss you mean to take, not the causse you claim to believe in, or the chain of eventss you accssidentally sset in motion."

He held out his hand. I took it and held my breath. We went up again, through the rocks.

And this time, when I could breathe again, my lungs filled with fresh outdoor air, seasoned with a little automobile exhaust. I opened my eyes.

We were in a parking lot, next to a statue of a man on a horse. I didn't recognize him, but I recognized the building looming above us. "It's Parliament. Parliament is built over a plague pit?"

He nodded. "Throughout London, whenever there iss a bleak and unuszed piecze of land, a legend growss that it iss above a plague pit. But the opposssite iss true: it iss the mosst lively placzes that are above pitss, for the energy of the dead never truly departss."

My head was spinning. The Great Fire and the Black Death and Guy Fawkes and my chapped hands all spun around in a giant whirl of good intentions with bad effects, and bad intentions with good effects, and it was all too big for me to grasp. I decided to take Inspector Sands's advice and just worry about my own actions. "You didn't have your men drag me here just to discuss morality. You want me to do something. What is it?"

"I would like you to wear a wire."

"A microphone? That seems so … unmagical."

"Not a microphone. A wire." He reached into a pocket and pulled out a rolled-up length of copper wire. "When you know where Lady Rossslyn and the drop of water are, placze one end of thiss wire on the ground and ssend a magical chargze through the other. My people will ssensse it. If you asssisst uss in capturing Lady Rossslyn, I think that will prove your innossensse to my ssupervissor."

I took the wire and tucked it into what remained of my jeans. I wasn't crazy about the idea of summoning Saltpetre Men on purpose, but I wanted to keep all my options open. "I need that magical charge you mentioned."

"No," Inspector Sands said. "Nobody will noticze you carrying a ssmall length of copper wire, but carrying a ssufiscziently powerful magical chargze would attract too much magical attention. Whatever Lady Rossslyn iss up to, you may be ssure it will involve powerful magic. It will be up to you to channel it to the wire."

Sands took my arm and steered me towards the gate that led out of the parking lot. The armed guard there nodded at him uninterestedly. I guess when you get whatever security clearance you need to guard Parliament, you learn that the government hires monsters.

Inspector Sands lingered in the shadow of the guard booth, out of sight of the pedestrians outside. He let go of my arm. "I am trussting you," he said. "Prove me right, or my ssupervissor will deal with you directly. You will not enjoy that. For now, you are free to go."

But go where? Lady Roslyn had been at the Monument a few hours before me. If she had started where the fire began, maybe she was tracing its entire course. And that meant I might be able to jump ahead of her.

"Where did the Great Fire end?"

"The Great Fire began in a bakery – and appropriately enough, it ended at Pye Corner."

I hailed a cab, and it pulled over. I would like to note that this was my first-ever hailing of a cab on my own. Historically speaking, maybe it wasn't as significant as my first-ever setting off a chain of magical catastrophes, but it still felt pretty cool.

Before I got in, I stuck my head in the front window just to be sure it wasn't Newfangled Troy. It wasn't. I don't know if I was disappointed or relieved.

I was about to climb in when I thought of something. I turned towards Inspector Sands. "How much is the cab fare to Pye Corner?"

"About fifteen poundss."

"So that means I would be about … let me see…"

I reached into my empty pocket. "About fifteen pounds short."

He produced some bills from his pocket. "Now you owe me your life, plusss fifteen poundss."

I took the bills and climbed into the cab. Then, before I closed the door, I leaned out and called to Inspector Sands.

"I haven't promised anything, you know," I told him.

His lips twisted into what was probably a smile. "I notissed," he said.

CHAPTER 28

*P*ye Corner looked like a normal London corner. The only hint that I was in the right place was a small golden statue of a fat little boy mounted in the wall. Under it was a stone inscription: THIS BOY IS IN MEMMORY PUT UP FOR THE LATE FIRE OF LONDON OCCASION'D BY THE SIN OF GLUTTONY.

Gluttony? Well, that was certainly an easier explanation than warring magical factions.

I stood there looking at the people passing by – men and women in business suits, moms and dads pushing baby carriages, tourists enjoying the summer afternoon – and I wondered if any of them knew the danger they were in. If I couldn't stop Lady Roslyn, the whole city might burn. And even if I did stop her, if I couldn't get the drop of water to Inspector Sands in time, the walls that held back the plague pit would be washed away.

I felt a tap on my shoulder. It was Little Ben. "Ooh, you had the same guess I did! I figured Lady Roslyn would be headed here."

I looked around. "Where's Oaroboarus?"

"We thought maybe we'd be a little more inconspicuous if he kept out of sight. Follow me."

As we crossed the street, Little Ben asked, "How did you escape the Saltpetre Men?"

I wasn't sure how much to tell him. If he was some kind of evil shape-shifter pretending to be a kid, then the less he knew, the better. And if he really *was* a lost kid, then telling him that his dad's team had once tried to blow up Parliament probably wouldn't cheer him up much. I decided to keep it vague. "They brought me to Inspector Sands. I told him I didn't steal anything, and he let me go."

We walked through an iron gate under a stone arch. There, standing guard over Little Ben's carpet-bag, was Oaroboarus, slouched despondently in the shadows. He'd be hard to miss for anybody walking through the arch, but at least he was out of sight of the street. He still had my sleeve clenched in his massive jaws.

"He wouldn't let go of it, the whole time," Little Ben said.

At the sound of his voice, Oaroboarus looked up and saw me. He bounded towards me so happily that I thought he was about to lick me. Then he got a grip on himself, gave a formal bow, and handed me my sleeve, followed by two cards.

MY MOST
HUMBLE APOLOGIES FOR
BEING UNABLE TO SAVE

YOU.

"Oh, please," I said. "You were amazingly brave." I wanted to pat him on the head, but I wondered if maybe he'd think that was undignified. He broke the awkward silence with a grunt. After only a few weeks in the country, I knew that was the sound an Englishman made when he was embarrassed by whatever you were talking about, so I dropped the subject. We all turned to look out at the street through the gate's iron grating.

"When do you think Lady Roslyn will show up?" Little Ben asked.

"I don't even know that she will," I said.

We stood and watched.

We waited.

In all the time since Mom had been snatched, this was the first chance I had had to just stand there and think, and I wasn't sure I liked it. All I *wanted* to think about was how great it would be to have Mom back, and how I was going to be a perfect daughter and never grump at her ever again. But whenever I tried to imagine that, my imagination would backtrack to the question of how I was going to get her back, and I still didn't have an answer. I mean, I knew I was going to have to defeat Lady Roslyn, and I knew I would need help to do that, but I still didn't know who I could trust.

Inspector Sands had said he was on my side, but his men had nearly killed me, and his supervisor apparently wanted me dead.

Little Ben seemed really friendly and enthusiastic, but I didn't know who he really was. Heck, even *he* didn't know who he was.

Oaroboarus had proven himself brave and loyal, but

he seemed at least as loyal to Little Ben, and if Little Ben turned out to be evil, I wasn't sure whose side Oaroboarus would take. Also, even if he took my side, the whole refusing-to-let-go-of-my-arm thing proved that he wouldn't necessarily do the smartest thing in a crisis.

I looked up to see Little Ben watching me. "Are you thinking about your mom?" he asked. "I think one of the reasons I've spent so much time studying my dad's file is, if I give myself time to just sit there, I get worried about everything." He gave me such a sympathetic and sincere smile that I immediately felt guilty for suspecting him of being an evil shape-shifter.

But then, isn't that exactly what an evil shape-shifter would want me to feel?

Before I could say anything back to him, Oaroboarus nudged me with a meaty shoulder. I looked through the grate and saw a taxi driving up to Pye Corner. Weirdly, it was driving backwards, swerving back and forth as it went. It drove halfway up onto the curb and screeched to a stop, and the driver stuck his head out the window.

I let out a little gasp. The driver was Backwards Head.

The taxi door opened, and Lady Roslyn climbed out.

My skin crawled. I hadn't seen her since she had disappeared with my mom, and I'd been wondering what I'd do when she finally reappeared. I wanted to run up and kick her, and I wanted to run screaming in the other direction, and I wanted to demand an explanation from her and then listen calmly while she made everything make sense.

But what I actually did was stay hidden behind the iron gate, taking deep breaths. If she saw me now, Lady Roslyn might hop back into the taxi and drive off, and I had no idea how I'd ever find her, or my mother, again.

Deep breaths.

Lady Roslyn reached into the cab and pulled out a long stick. Then she pulled out a ceramic plate with high wavy edges.

"Is that … a pie plate?" I asked.

Neither Oaroboarus nor Little Ben answered my question, because Lady Roslyn answered it for us. "The pie, JB," she called to Backwards Head. "While it's still warm, please."

His name is JB? I thought. *Everybody else in this magical world has a long name with at least one adjective, and the guy with the backwards head only gets two letters?*

Backwards Head – no, JB – handed Lady Roslyn a pie through the cab window.

Or, at least, he tried to hand it to her. He couldn't quite crane his head around to see where his arms were going, and he nearly dropped the pie on the pavement.

Lady Roslyn snatched it from him, put it on the plate, and then screwed the plate onto the edge of the long stick.

She lifted up the stick until the pie was right in front of the statue's mouth.

The chubby golden boy stood there.

Then his arms began to tremble, like he was trying to move them for the first time in decades. Slowly at first, they stretched out towards the pie. Then he snatched it with his two golden hands and whisked it up to his golden mouth. He wolfed the whole thing down with about as much dignity as you'd expect from a pudgy two-year-old who hadn't eaten in centuries.

As soon as he finished, his hands dropped and he froze again. The only sign that he had come to life was the red cherry filling smeared across his golden face and the fallen pie tin slowly revolving on the pavement.

With a rumble we could hear all the way across the street, the inscribed stone under the statue swung open. Lady Roslyn stepped inside and vanished, and JB followed her.

The stone started to rumble shut.

CHAPTER 29

ran.

As I crossed the pavement, I knocked over a tourist, sending his burrito flying under the wheel of a passing car.

I sprinted across the street. I could hear the cars screeching to a stop moments before they squashed me as flat as the burrito, but I didn't bother looking at them. I kept my eyes on that closing stone door.

I made it across the street, but the stone door was almost shut and it was a good ten feet away, and I had just realized I wasn't going to make it when Oaroboarus did a kind of scooping leap that hoisted me onto his back next to Little Ben, and the three of us flew through the air.

We shot through the door, and Little Ben and I tumbled off as Oaroboarus landed. The door clicked shut behind us, locking out the daylight.

A dim light flickered on – along with everything else in his carpetbag, Little Ben had a flashlight. He shined it on a ramp that curved down into the darkness. There was no sign of Lady Roslyn or backwards-headed JB or anybody else.

We crept downwards along the ramp.

As Little Ben's light skimmed along it, I noticed that the bottom of the wall had been worn smooth in a groove that spiralled the whole way down the ramp. "What do you think made that?" I asked.

"Maybe people's feet, wearing it down over the centuries?"

"But it's on the wall. *Your* feet don't scrape the wall as you walk. *Mine* don't. Why would anybody else's? Unless this was a secret lair for people wearing clown shoes."

We reached the bottom, and in the dim light of the flashlight's beam, I could see a long brick vault lined with small, arched side rooms. "Oooh, I know where we are," Little Ben whispered. "I've seen a picture of this. It's the basement of the Fortune of War."

"What's that?"

"It's an old pub that used to be here. It was right

next to a graveyard and across the street from the hospital, and the traffic between those two places went through here."

"You mean people who died in the hospital, getting taken to the graveyard?"

"No!" Little Ben said. "The other way around. Doctors needed bodies to practise doing surgery. They'd buy them from people called Resurrection Men, which was just a fancy way of saying grave robber. They'd store the bodies in those nooks on the wall, then they'd meet the doctors upstairs in the pub to negotiate a price."

It made sense, in a grim, people-used-to-be-pretty-sick kind of way. "That's why there are those grooves in the wall on the ramp down," I said, "It *was* people's feet. But it was the feet of corpses, scraping the wall as they got dragged up and down. Which is almost as creepy as clowns."

Oaroboarus grunted quietly, bringing my attention back to the task at hand. We had reached the end of the vault, where a rusty metal door hung open on its hinges. Through it, we could hear echoing footsteps. We stopped and held our breaths. The footsteps got quieter – Lady Roslyn and JB were headed away from us. We slipped through the door.

We were in another long vault, but instead of little

brick cubbies, this one was lined with narrow brick rooms, each one covered by an iron grating and a locked door.

"Are those jail cells?" I asked.

Little Ben nodded. "Yup. In addition to the hospital, the pub, and the graveyard, there was a jail on this street – a famous one called Newgate Prison. It was all part of the same cycle. They'd be locked up here while they were waiting to be hanged. Then they'd be buried in the graveyard, and then they'd get dug up and sold to the hospital."

"The whole industry was in one place," I said. "Nice. It was like Silicon Valley for sickos."

Little Ben looked confused. "What's Silicon Valley?"

"Seriously?"

"If it's not in my dad's files, I don't know anything about it."

I didn't get a chance to respond. A voice whispered, "Hurry!" in my ear, and I jumped, because I recognized it immediately. It was Lady Roslyn.

CHAPTER 30

$\mathcal{M}$y pulse racing, I looked frantically around, but she was nowhere to be seen.

THESE WALLS ECHO FIERCELY.

AND IF WE CAN HEAR HER ...

I nodded silently and held a finger up to my lips to show I understood: if we could hear her, she could hear us. Fortunately, if I was only just hearing her now, we must have only just reached the echo-y bit, and she wouldn't have heard Little Ben and me whispering.

I hoped.

We tiptoed forwards.

Her words reached me again, echoing from somewhere ahead in the darkness: "What is taking you so long?"

There was a muffled sound, as if somebody was responding but happened to be standing in slightly the wrong place for the echo to bring his words to me.

Whatever he said, Lady Roslyn didn't sound happy as she hissed, "Then you should have brought a mirror, you fool."

Ahead, through another iron doorway, we could see someone else's flashlight in the darkness. Little Ben turned his off, and we crept onwards.

As we got closer, we could make out Lady Roslyn standing impatiently while JB tried to pick the lock of a big iron cage. I could see why he was having a hard time, with his wrong-way face pressed into a brick corner and his arms pointing the other way.

"Almost got it," JB said as clearly as he could with his lips mushed up against the brick.

If they almost had whatever they were looking for, that meant they'd soon be turning around and heading back our way. I touched Little Ben's sleeve and pointed at one of the cells next to us. Its bars had rusted off, making a hole that even Oaroboarus could squeeze through. We slid in, just as we heard JB say "Ah-haha!" triumphantly.

The cage door he had been picking swung open. As he stepped aside, I got a glimpse of what was in it. It looked like somebody had made a beehive out of clay, then dripped splotches of red paint on it.

Whatever it was, Lady Roslyn was really happy to see it. She let out a cackle and reached out to touch it, but then she shrieked in pain and jumped back.

"Remarkable," she said. "Still hot after all these years."

She fished in her pocket and pulled out a thick, elaborately embroidered cloth and a rag. She held out the rag to JB, but since his face was pointed the other way, he didn't notice. She sighed and thrust it into his hand.

With Lady Roslyn using her embroidered cloth like a pot holder and JB using the rag, they hoisted the beehive thingy up and staggered off.

"Watch it!" Lady Roslyn yelled. "Careful! Say, do you suppose the one of us who has her head facing in the right direction ought to lead? You do? Splendid. That's better. Now, let us hurry, before the Bunny Tears come."

Bunny Tears? She sounded as if it was something

pretty frightening, but I couldn't see being scared of bunny tears.

There wasn't time to think about it much. As they staggered closer, I shrank back as far into the darkness as I could – but that wasn't very far, given how shallow the cell was. I held my breath.

Lady Roslyn and JB passed by, grunting and muttering. I could feel the heat coming off the beehive, and I could somehow feel the power of it, too. But I couldn't figure out what it actually was until I had to take in a little breath, and I smelled something surprisingly nice: freshly baked bread.

She was carrying the oven that had started the Great Fire.

No wonder the thing radiated power. With that, and the Fire Hook, and the charged drop of water, she could... Well, actually, I had no idea what she could do. But I was pretty sure she wasn't going to use the oven to make cupcakes for my mother. I had a sudden urge to tackle her, but I held myself back. Even if we managed to subdue her and JB, she'd never tell us where she had stashed Mom, and I might never get her back.

I watched Lady Roslyn and JB vanish into the darkness. Even when they were gone, the delicious bread smell lingered. And I wasn't the only one who smelled it, because Little Ben let out a loud, moaning "Mmmmmmmmmmmm."

I turned to him and held my finger to my lips – and discovered he was doing the same to me. He wasn't the one who'd made the noise.

We looked at Oaroboarus, who shook his head.

"Mmmmmmmmmmmm," moaned the voice again. "Mmmm... Mmmm..."

That's when I realized it wasn't one voice – it was many.

Coming from the darkness of the cells all around us.

Darkness that was beginning to glow faintly.

In the glow of our own cell, I could see a dim face beginning to form.

No, that wasn't right – the face *was* the glow.

It solidified, from a faint face-shaped mist to something so clear, I could see the dry cracks in the parched lips, and the greying stubble on the chin, and the desperate look in the eyes. "Guv'nor," whispered the lips. "Is that ... *buns* I smell?"

The rest of the mist was taking shape, too, into a gaunt, glowing body, hung with rags. It stepped towards me – no, it *glided* towards me – and I backed away on trembling legs. I couldn't take my eyes off the glowing face, but in the corner of my vision, I could see Little

Ben and Oaroboarus backing away, too.

"Buns, guv'nor?" the glowing face pleaded. "Buns for me, and sixpence for my widow?"

It wasn't the Bunny Tears Lady Roslyn was afraid of, I realized. It was the Bun Eaters.

"I'm very sorry," I told him as clearly as I could, although my voice was shaking and my mouth suddenly felt as dry as his looked. "I don't have any food or any money."

"But I smell buns," the Bun Eater said. "And I'm hungry. So hungry." And from the cells around us, I heard murmured voices joining him: *So hungry. So very hungry.*

He took a deep breath, as if inhaling the bread smell that lingered from the oven. And then he took an even deeper breath, and I could feel scents swirling off *me.* From my skin wafted the salty smell of the tuna I had eaten, and the yeasty smell of the bread that had held it, and the sweetcorn that had been mixed with it. And not just my most recent meal. I suddenly knew that to a dead man, I must smell like cookies and fruit, and sodas that hadn't even been invented when he had died.

He licked his lips and stretched out a glowing hand towards me.

From the cells around us, more glowing figures

were gliding out of the shadows.

If you're wondering why I didn't climb onto Oaro-boarus and let him whisk me out of there, well, you try looking into the hungry eyes of a dozen starving ghosts sliding towards you, and see how rationally *you* plan your exit strategy.

Me? I turned around and ran.

I didn't scream, which I'd like to say was because I had enough presence of mind to realize that Lady Roslyn might hear me. But really, I was just too terri-fied to force out any noise.

Oaroboarus ran right past me without trying to scoop me up, and I could hear Little Ben puffing be-hind me, so I'm guessing neither of them was carefully plotting out the calmest response, either.

We ran through the first iron door and into the room with the corpse cubbies, which were glowing with the same eerie light. In the cubbies, Bun Eaters stirred, sat upright, sniffed, and began to moan.

I kept running.

We ran up the spiral ramp, and when we got to the stone door onto the street, Oaroboarus smashed right into it without stopping. It flew open, and we sprinted into the sunlight.

We could still hear the moaning from inside, but it didn't get any closer. Whatever Bun Eaters were,

I guess they didn't come into the light.

For a moment, we stood there, hunched over and panting, ignoring the stares from the passers-by who had just seen a giant pig smash through a stone door.

Then we heard car tyres screeching. We looked up and saw JB's taxi zooming away from us, backwards.

CHAPTER 31

By now, Little Ben and I had calmed down enough to do the smart thing. We leapt onto Oaroboarus's back, and we were off.

Ahead of us, the taxi drove wildly, screeching back and forth, just barely avoiding cars going in both directions.

That wasn't exactly good for public safety, but it did make it easy to follow the cab. At least, until Lady Roslyn spotted us.

She was sitting in the backseat of a turned-around taxi, so she had a great view of everything behind her, and she would probably have seen us sooner if she hadn't been so busy yelling at JB. But finally, she had to stop for breath. That's when she glanced out her windscreen and found herself looking right at us. Her face turned bright red. She yelled something new at JB, and he floored it.

The taxi shot forwards – erm, backwards, I mean – not even bothering to dodge other cars, which forced the drivers around it to skid madly. A fancy SUV screeched to the right to avoid the taxi, then screeched back to the left so it didn't crash into an oncoming car, but that took it straight into our path.

Oaroboarus leapt over it.

I looked down at the SUV as we sailed above it, right into the eyes of the astonished driver. His jaw was hanging open, like he couldn't believe what was happening to him. I knew how he felt.

We slammed back down onto the ground, cars careening around us, and JB swerved to the left.

That happened to be the wrong direction down a one-way street.

Oaroboarus leapt over another oncoming car, then another, but this time, he misjudged the landing a little and went crashing into a huge flowerpot on the pavement, shattering it and sending a shower of dirt and azaleas onto the terrified patrons of an outdoor café.

"Sorry!" I yelled.

Oaroboarus jumped back into the road, dodged a truck, hurdled over a motorcycle, and then, as the road became a two-way street again, merged back into the correct lane. This was the responsible driving choice (or, I guess, the responsible pigging choice), but the problem was, JB was still driving in the wrong lane, which meant other cars had to keep skidding into our lane to dodge him, which meant Oaroboarus had to veer back into the wrong lane to dodge *them*, which put him right in the path of a car that was bouncing down off the pavement where it had driven to avoid JB's taxi, so the only place for Oaroboarus to jump was onto the pavement where the car had come from.

And that would have been fine, except that when the car was on the pavement, it had sideswiped a row of red telephone boxes and almost knocked them over, leaving them just barely balanced on one side, so when Oaroboarus's hooves pounded the ground next to them, they tipped over completely.

They came toppling down towards us.

Little Ben and I ducked, which only bought us about a tenth of a second, but fortunately in that tenth of a second, Oaroboarus tilted back towards the road, and the crashing phone boxes missed us.

At this point, Oaroboarus must have had enough of dodging cars, because he jumped on top of a bus, his hooves thundering along the metal roof, then jumped straight onto the top of a fast-moving van, bounding briefly down to the ground before leaping up onto a row of parked cars and running along atop them.

I thought this was a pretty good approach, since it put us in the path of a lot fewer oncoming cars. Of course, the people who owned the parked cars we were denting probably wouldn't have agreed with me.

Throughout most of this crazy chase, the white dome of St Paul's Cathedral had loomed above the buildings we passed, getting closer and closer all the time. Now we were nearly there. *Of course*, I thought. *Lady Roslyn is collecting magical items for some sort of uncanny ritual. It makes sense that she'd want to do it in the most impressive sacred building in town.*

But instead of turning right towards St Paul's, JB's taxi took a sudden left and smashed through a metal barricade with NO VEHICLES written on it.

On the other side of the barrier was a pedestrian street filled with market stalls and shoppers, all screaming and diving for cover as the taxi smashed through.

Oaroboarus leapt off the roof of a parked car and onto the roof of one of the market stalls. It turns out that market stalls are not quite as solid as cars. This one collapsed under us, smashing everything in it.

That included a lot of umbrellas, but not any people, since the umbrella-seller had dived for cover just in time. Still, it was way too close. It looked like we had two choices. We could smash on through the crowd like JB, not caring who got hurt – or we could just watch helplessly as the taxi vanished.

Oaroboarus chose an option I hadn't considered: he barrelled right through the stalls, swerving every once in a while to dodge the occasional foolish seller who hadn't jumped out of the way. As Oaroboarus's hooves shattered the display tables into wooden mush, Little Ben and I found ourselves riding through a blizzard of off-brand batteries, tie-dyed shawls, and Union Jack underpants.

Finally, we emerged from the market right behind the taxi. Oaroboarus stayed close behind it as we zoomed past the Tower of London and onto Tower Bridge.

The bridge was jammed with cars, so JB drove up onto the wide pavement, which didn't leave any room for the group of tourists who had been walking there, forcing them to jump into the road, where, fortunately, traffic was at a standstill. The tourists were safe …

… except for one grey-haired woman who froze, panicked, and then stumbled the wrong way, toppling over the side of the bridge and plunging into the river

Thames. She spun as she fell, and I thought for sure the impact would kill her, but she somehow entered the water cleanly. For several terrifying seconds, she stayed below, and then she fought her way to the surface.

Oaroboarus skidded to a stop. He looked at the taxi disappearing off into the distance. He looked down at the woman desperately clawing at the water as the current swept her away. He was too stubborn to let the taxi get away, but he was too stubborn to let the woman drown.

I figured I'd better resolve the dilemma for him. "You have to save that woman," I yelled, slapping him on the head as Little Ben and I slid off him.

He shook himself off, as if emerging from a trance, and leapt over the railing. With a huge splash, he plunged into the river, then rose up to grab the astonished woman's shirt in his jaws. As he paddled with her towards the shore, I looked up and saw the taxi exit the bridge and vanish around the corner. I wondered if my chances of finding Mom had vanished with it.

"We have to figure out where Lady Roslyn is going," I told Little Ben. "She went the opposite way from the Houses of Parliament, and she passed right by St Paul's Cathedral. She must be going someplace more important than either of them."

"Oooooh. OOOH! There's only one place that can be," Little Ben said. "She's going to the Crossness sewage pumping station."

PART
THREE

CHAPTER 32

$\mathcal{J}$ smelled the sewage plant before I saw it. Somehow, the scent was even worse than it had been inside the actual sewer pipes. There, the odour had been so over-powering that I just got used to it. Here, it kept getting fainter or stronger, depending on how the wind blew, so that I could never quite forget about it. It made my stomach squirm.

Or maybe that was fear.

OK, it was definitely fear. But the odour didn't help.

A chain-link fence surrounded the Crossness Pumping Station. Oaroboarus leapt over it. Little Ben and I climbed down, and I looked around. It was a blandly modern utility complex, with wan grass growing between clean, dull buildings. There were no guards and no workers in sight. That was probably just because today was Sunday, and not because Lady Roslyn had done something horrible to them, probably the same thing she was about to do to my mother—

Hold on, Hyacinth. Calm down. I took a deep breath. Then I gagged a little and decided that henceforth, all deep breaths would go through my mouth and not my nose.

A gravel road led through the complex. I pointed to it, then put my finger to my lips. Little Ben and Oaroboarus nodded, and the three of us crept along, walking on the grass next to the road, rather than on the noisy gravel.

We turned a corner and came upon a building that looked totally out of place. It must have been a hundred years older than all the others. It was smaller, and made out of grey and black brick. The stones set above its large, arched windows might once have been orange, but now they had the same dirty, faded look as the rest of the building.

From the other side of the building, I thought I could hear Lady Roslyn's voice, but I couldn't make out what she was saying. I looked around for cover, but there were only a few scattered trees. I stuck as close to them as I could, although given that I was being followed by a giant pig, hiding behind the occasional scrawny tree probably wasn't going to make us less conspicuous. I just had to hope that Lady Roslyn wouldn't come this way.

We made it to the edge of the old building, and I peered around the corner. Around the other side, Lady Roslyn and JB were wheeling a large, industrial-looking machine out of a side building. I jerked my head back and waited there as Lady Roslyn's curses and JB's grunts and the machine's squeaky wheels grew closer and closer. Then they were right around the corner, no more than a few feet from us. I held my breath.

The curses and the grunts and the squeaks faded away. They had gone inside.

I counted to ten, then dashed around the corner, Little Ben and Oaroboarus right behind me.

Inside the building, long skylights let the daylight into a wide, low entry hall with no furniture, leaving no place to hide. I hesitated at the entrance.

Somehow I could sense that Mom was nearby. I took a deep breath and ran as silently as I could towards the archway at the other end of the hall.

As I got closer, I could hear Lady Roslyn's voice again. I couldn't quite make out her words, but it sounded like she was chanting.

When we reached the archway, we stopped, crouching in the shadows there, and peered into the next room. As quiet as I was trying to be, I couldn't help gasping.

The main hall of the Crossness Pumping Station was a madhouse of ironwork. There were tall red columns topped by ornate green curlicues holding up arches overflowing with yellow and green swirls. Some of it was rusting and falling apart, and some of it must have been recently restored, with brand-new royal red and tree-green paint.

It was like a merry-go-round had exploded inside a palace.

And in the middle of it all, Lady Roslyn knelt on a floor of iron grating, chanting strange words: "Lord Lucan. Viscount Sydney. Viscount Eversly. Lord Duffering."

"I know those names," Little Ben whispered. "In the 1800s, they had a big opening ceremony for this building, and they invited all the most famous and powerful people in the country. She's reciting the guest list. But why?"

"Hmmm…" I whispered back. "Remember what you said, about how ninety per cent of British life makes sense, but it's the crazy ten per cent where the magic is? Well, it's crazy to make a sewage processing plant this beautiful. They couldn't have built it to just process waste. If all the sewers run through here, then so do all the magical rivers. Maybe this was the centre of magical control. And if the magic of the rivers can inspire people – well, maybe it works both ways. Maybe if you gather all the artists and leaders, having so many inspired people in one place generates magical power."

"That explains why they invited them a hundred and fifty years ago," Little Ben whispered. "But now they're dead. They can't help her tonight!"

"Remember the Bun Eaters? Just because you're dead doesn't mean you can't get involved. The oven summoned the ghosts of the people who had been in the jail. Maybe she brought it here to summon the spirits of those first visitors."

And, in fact, as Lady Roslyn continued reciting names, I could see the air beginning to take on a familiar glow. It wasn't as bright and vivid as it had been in the underground cells where the oven had been stored – but it was still enough to send a shiver down my spine.

Oaroboarus gave me a nudge and pointed his hoof at something near Lady Roslyn's feet. I squinted and saw what he was gesturing at. Something was dripping from the ironwork high above her head and passing through the iron grating at her feet.

"What is it?" I asked.

Oaroboarus leaned forwards and took a deep sniff through his enormous snout.

BLOOD.

Back when they were trying to kidnap me, Richard the Raker had started to say something about my bloodline before Longface Lucky cut him off. I'd thought that he meant it as a figure of speech, and that he was just talking about my family heritage. But as I watched the blood drip from the ceiling, I realized he must have meant it literally, too. My family had some connection to London's magical rivers, and that connection ran right through our veins. And that meant there was only one person whose blood that could be.

I reached out and grabbed the nearest iron column, because if I didn't hold on tight, I was going to run right over and take a swing at Lady Roslyn, and that wouldn't do any good. If I wanted to rescue my mother before she bled to death, I was going to have to be subtle.

Forcing myself to stay calm, I looked around and assessed the situation. There was a circle of iron columns around Lady Roslyn. If we stayed in the shadows behind them, we could get past her and make it unseen to the steps that led up to the next floor.

I crept forwards, lifting each foot gently so it wouldn't clank on the iron grating. Every muscle in my body was screaming at me to run, but I held them back, and went step by gentle step. I had the sense that, behind me, Little Ben and Oaroboarus were doing the same thing, but I was so focused on moving forwards, it didn't occur to me to look back.

We moved closer to Lady Roslyn, and closer still. I could hear the faint *plink* as each drop of blood – of *my mom's blood* – hit the iron floor and dripped through.

"Mr A. T. B. Beresford Hope," Lady Roslyn said. *Plink.*

Now we were within two feet of her. Immersed in the shadows, we were safely out of her sight – but JB must be somewhere nearby. Maybe he was patrolling the area. Wherever he was, he could come back and spot us at any moment.

But still we crept on, slowly, slowly.

We passed Lady Roslyn and headed towards the narrow spiral staircase that led up into the darkness, towards where my mom must lie bleeding.

Plink. Plink.

I needed to be patient. *Plink.*

But that was my mother's blood dripping down. How much did she have left? *Plink.*

I picked up the pace. Now my feet made the faintest echo on the iron floor. I prayed that Lady Roslyn would be too immersed in her chant to hear it.

She kept going. "Sir John S. Pakington." *Plink.*

At the staircase, I put my foot on the lowest iron step, then lowered my weight onto it, as slowly and carefully as I could bear. It squeaked softly. I paused.

"Mr Heywood, engineer to the City Commission of Sewers." *Plink.*

I kept climbing. Little Ben followed me, with Oaroboarus behind him. Oaroboarus had somehow managed to tread silently until now, but when he reached the stairs, his hooves made a little *ting!* on every iron step. I winced each time, but Lady Roslyn kept chanting.

"The Honorable Colonel Luke White." *Plink. Ting!* "Sir Colman O'Loghlen." *Plink. Ting!*

At the top of the steps, I stuck my head just up high enough to peer into the iron mezzanine above, and I saw three things.

The first thing was the big machine that Lady Roslyn and JB had carried in. It was some kind of industrial drill, but instead of a drill bit on the end, it had King Charles's Fire Hook attached to it. The machine's whirring engine made the pointy bit of the Fire Hook spin around rapidly.

The second thing I saw was my mom, eyes closed but still breathing, lying on a table below the machine. The Fire Hook was boring into her arm with an amazingly gentle touch, teasing out drop after drop of blood.

And the heck with the third thing, because at that point, I was running up the steps as fast as I had ever run, towards the machine and my mom, completely forgetting about being quiet or hiding, which was too bad, because right when I was in the middle of my frantic, loud-clanging run, I finally noticed the third thing.

It was JB. He was sitting next to the machine, slowly lowering the drill onto Mom's arm.

I felt a moment of panic, then a moment of relief when I realized his back was to me, and then a moment of even greater panic when I realized the one place you couldn't hide from JB was behind his back.

CHAPTER 33

*W*ith a roar, JB leapt to his feet and ran at me, backwards. Then he looked up at something over my head, and suddenly, he looked as frightened as I felt.

I tracked his eyes upwards and saw Oaroboarus above me in mid-leap. He crashed into JB, sending him tumbling.

I ran to the machine and pulled with all my might, trying to remove the spinning Fire Hook from Mom's arm. I couldn't budge it.

Frantically, I searched for an off switch, but there wasn't one. There was a long electrical cord trailing out of the machine, though. I grabbed it and yanked hard. It came flying out of the socket in the wall, and the machine whirred to a stop.

By now, Little Ben had caught up to me. "I can't lift this up," I told him. He grabbed one part of the metal arm holding the Fire Hook, and I grabbed another, and we strained and pulled and grunted, and finally it swung up.

"Mom! Wake up! It's me. It's Hyacinth! Wake up!" I shook her shoulder gently, then harder, but she still wouldn't wake up.

What had Lady Roslyn said? *Waking her will be simple when the time is right.* But how were you supposed to wake somebody from an enchanted sleep—

Oh. Right.

I bent forwards and kissed her. (No, it was NOT on the lips. I was perfectly happy to wade through a massive river of poop to get Mom back, but I wasn't going to do anything *gross*.)

As my lips brushed her forehead, Mom's eyes flickered for a moment, then opened.

"Hyacinth?" she murmured, smiling up at me.

There was so much I wanted to say, I couldn't even decide where to begin. Finally, I settled on a key fact. "I love you, Mom," I told her.

"That's nice," she said dozily. "Can you get me up in fifteen minutes?"

"NO!" I said, and I guess I said it pretty intensely,

because her eyes popped completely open and she grabbed my arm.

"What's wrong?" she said as I helped her to her feet. "Where are we? Why is that man's head backwards? Is he about to stab a pig? Have you eaten? You look hungry."

I whirled around. JB had somehow clambered on top of Oaroboarus, who was bucking wildly, trying to throw him. And JB had a knife. And he was holding it up, about to strike.

I jumped at him, grabbing his arm, but I only slowed him down a little bit. He was just too strong. Little Ben grabbed on to his wrist, too, but even that only slowed him down a little. The knife moved closer to Oaroboarus's back … closer…

And then another hand grabbed JB, stopping the movement of the knife immediately. "That will be quite enough," Lady Roslyn said, snatching the dagger from his hand. "You will not stab that boar."

My jaw dropped. Was she somehow on my side after all?

She handed JB a thin wire. "Strangle him instead," she said.

JB grinned his disturbing sideways grin. Then he whipped the wire around Oaroboarus's neck and started pulling. Little Ben and I tried to yank him off, but it was no use. Oaroboarus was choking and turning purple. His kicks and jumps became less and less energetic. I pounded my fists against JB's back, but he didn't even seem to notice.

Lady Roslyn had saved Oaroboarus from stabbing only to have him strangled, and now he was going to die, and there was nothing I could—

Wait a minute. *Why* did she save him from being stabbed? She was clearly happy to have him dead. And based on what she had been doing to my mom, she had no objection to drawing blood with sharp pokey things, so why—

Ohhhhhhh. I figured it out.

"Little Ben! What would you do to save Oaroboarus?"

He stopped his futile wrestling with JB and looked up at me, tears streaming down his face. "Anything!"

"Then give me your hand."

I dragged him over to the Fire Hook and held his hand beneath it, as if I were about to impale him on it. Then I called out to Lady Roslyn, "Call off JB!"

She stared at me in disbelief. "Or what?"

"Or I'll give Little Ben a really bad cut."

She snorted. "You're trying to intimidate me by threatening somebody on your side? An interesting strategy."

"No, what's interesting is that you didn't want Oaroboarus stabbed. The only reason I can think of is, you don't want his blood mixing with all that blood from my mom that you've so carefully collected. There's something special about my family's blood, isn't there? Well, Little Ben isn't in my family." I looked at Little Ben, and he nodded. I moved his hand closer to the Fire Hook's sharp edge, keeping my eyes locked on Lady Roslyn's.

"You're right, as far as it goes," she said. "I wouldn't want his dirty, common blood contaminating your mother's lovely pure stuff." Lady Roslyn grabbed Mom and pressed the knife she had taken from JB against her neck.

Until now, Mom had been watching everything with a slightly drowsy confusion. Now her eyes opened wide with fear. "Please," she whispered, too terrified to say more.

Lady Roslyn ignored her. "Therefore, Hyacinth, if you spill a single drop of Little Ben's blood, I'll have to overwhelm it with quite a lot of your mother's blood to compensate. Are you willing to spill more of your friend's blood than I am of your mother's?"

"You're bluffing," I said, trying to sound a lot more confident than I felt. "If you wanted all her blood at once, you'd have killed her already. I think you need a slow, steady flow for whatever magic you're doing."

Lady Roslyn held the knife even tighter against Mom's throat, so that the slightest additional pressure would cut the skin. I dug my fingernails into the palm of my hand just as tightly, trying to stay calm. It was not easy. Mom was now making little frightened whimpers.

Lady Roslyn smiled at me. "I'd certainly *prefer* a steady flow of blood. Unleashing too much power at once would have unpredictable consequences. It might grant me the power I seek without the trouble of a long and difficult ceremony. Or it might destroy London and kill everybody in it. But if the unimaginable magical powers of London don't belong to somebody as reasonable and selfless as me, I genuinely think we'd all be better off dead. Here, let's not waste any time. I give you my unambiguous word of honour, unbreakable in the presence of all this magic: if you so much as prick Little Ben's finger, I will cut your mother's throat wide open."

Mom finally choked out a few words. "Hyacinth, honey, *what is happening?*"

"It's OK, Mom," I told her. "We're saving you." I let go of Little Ben's hand, and we both stepped away from the Fire Hook.

While Lady Roslyn and I had been negotiating,

JB had carried on throttling Oaroboarus. I watched in horror as Oaroboarus gave one last, desperate buck, then collapsed with a mighty *clang*. I wanted to rush to him, but there was still the whole knife-to-my-mother's throat thing going on.

"You told me you were on the side of good!" I yelled at Lady Roslyn. "You said your family had a strict code of ethics, passed on from generation to generation!"

"I spoke the truth," Lady Roslyn said. "I would never take a life unless it was strictly necessary. I'm not doing this to hurt you, Hyacinth. I've got nothing against your mother, and believe it or not, I actually like you quite a bit. But this is necessary for the greater good. While the Inheritors of Order controlled the rivers' power, the steam engine was invented, slavery was abolished, Keats wrote his poetry, and the British Museum opened. Then we lost control, and what happened? The Crimean War and the Sepoy Mutiny."

"The Crimean War, *and* Darwin discovered evolution, and Charles Dickens wrote *Great Expectations*," Little Ben said. He was still crying, but it seemed like nothing could stop his memory for facts. "Good and bad things happen in every era. It doesn't prove anything!"

Lady Roslyn shrugged. "We'll settle this debate soon enough. Within an hour, I will control the secret rivers. And you'll see: Britain will enter a new golden age. We'll—"

She kept talking, but honestly, I could not have cared less about this particular debate if I had tried. I didn't know how the steam engine was invented or slavery was abolished, but I was pretty sure it hadn't involved bleeding innocent moms to death. And maybe Charles Dickens wrote *Great Expectations* while wearing a top hat to preserve his precious inspiration or maybe he didn't.

But. While Lady Roslyn was caught up in her argument with Little Ben, she had loosened the knife against Mom's throat just a little, which let me calm down just a little. And that let me think a little more clearly about the situation.

JB was a threat, but I knew from past experience that I could dodge him if I had to. And Lady Roslyn had already admitted that she'd rather not cut Mom's throat. So if I lunged for her, she'd hesitate for at least a second.

I hoped.

So I lunged.

That was obviously not what Lady Roslyn was expecting, because she stopped mid-sentence and stared at me for one brief moment, which was just long enough for me to grab her arm with all my might and pull it a little bit loose. "Slide free, Mom!" I yelled.

For once, Mom listened to me. She slipped down, out of Lady Roslyn's grasp.

Lady Roslyn lashed out at me. I stumbled backwards, the tip of the knife a fraction of an inch away from my skin. Out of the corner of my eye, I could see JB lumbering backwards towards me, but I wasn't worried about him –

– until two hooves slammed into my back, making it explode with pain and sending me tumbling forward, just as JB spun around and grabbed me. He held me tight to his chest, and I got a look at where those hooves had come from.

It was a unicorn. There was a jagged, broken stub on top of his head, and the rest of the horn hung from a chain around his neck.

"You're … what was your name? Sirion, right?" I said.

The unicorn just glared at me.

"It's probably a good thing we can't hear what he's thinking," JB chortled. I struggled as hard as I could, but he had me in a tight grip.

CHAPTER 34

*J*kicked and I screamed, but in minutes, Little Ben and I had been dragged down the spiral staircase and tied to an ornate iron railing. Lady Roslyn hadn't even tried to move Oaroboarus. She just had JB tie up his legs, which I hoped was a good sign. If Oaroboarus was dead, they probably wouldn't have bothered tying him up, right? I was going to assume that was the case. *Please let that be the case.*

Through the holes in the iron ceiling above us, I could see Lady Roslyn tying Mom to the drill. "Please, let us go," Mom said. Lady Roslyn ignored her. "Fine," Mom said. "Then let Hyacinth go, and that little boy. They're just children. They – ouch!" She winced as Lady Roslyn pushed the tip of the Fire Hook into her arm.

Plink. I shivered. Mom's blood was once again dripping down from above.

Lady Roslyn strode down the spiral staircase. "I believe we've wasted enough time," she said. She knelt down and went back to listing names. "Alderman Mechi. Lord Claud Hamilton."

I struggled with the ropes around my wrists, but they wouldn't budge. Little Ben leaned over and whispered, "You don't need to—" He stopped and looked over at Sirion, who was guarding us with an intent, hostile expression. "Can that unicorn hear us?"

Good question. I figured there was only one way to find out. "Hey, Sirion," I whispered. "Unicorns drool. Lions rule!" Sirion didn't react. He just kept staring at us with the same focused expression. Was he reading my mind? *Hey, Sirion, remember how I broke your horn? That was fun,* I thought. He still didn't react.

I turned back to Little Ben. "He's used to communicating telepathically, so I don't think his ears are that good. And with his broken horn, I don't think his mind-powers work."

"Great. In that case, I was going to say, I think I can untie you. Should I—"

"Not yet," I whispered back. "Wait until he looks away."

By now, Lady Roslyn was reaching the end of her guest list. "... Mr James McCann, Mr John Locke, and Mr S. Gurney, I welcome you in the name of the queen. I summon the power of your witness! I summon the power of the rivers! I summon *you*, Queen Victoria. I call you to life!"

The spectral glow in the air intensified. I held my breath, ready for the ghost of the queen to appear. But instead, the glow flowed to a massive iron machine in the corner of the building and vanished inside its gears. The machine churned to life. I never thought of machines as having names, but apparently, this one was named Queen Victoria. It let out a tremendous *Hssss* and steam began to belch out of it – glowing steam, as though it were made out of that same strange ghostly energy.

Queen Victoria was a steam engine.

A massive wheel inched to life, turning slowly at first, then more and more steadily. It hissed again and let out a *kchick chick chick*, like there were dozens of gears rattling inside it.

The engine's iron parts shone brighter and brighter, until its rich red paint looked like fire.

Plink. Mom's blood still dripped downwards – but now it glowed, too, so that each drop was like a little light bulb falling through the air. *Plink.*

And it wasn't just Mom's blood. Everything that was touched by the billowing cloud of spectral steam became transformed. The parts of the building that had been rusty unrusted themselves. Where the paint had been flaking, it smoothed out and once again gleamed royal red and forest green, and then began to glow with its own light.

Soon, the billowing cloud had spread to the opposite corner of the building, where another old steam engine sat unmoving.

"I summon you, Prince Consort!" Lady Roslyn called, and that machine let out its own *HSSSSS*. *Kchick chick chick*. It started turning, slowly, so that at first, it was out of sync with the Queen Victoria engine, and the two of them together sounded like a syncopated rhythm of steel and metal. Then the Prince Consort got up to full speed, and the two engines spoke with one voice, loud enough to hurt my eardrums on the *HSSSSS*.

As terrified as I was, it was an amazing show. And I wasn't the only one to think so – Sirion was staring at the throbbing steam engines, too.

Which meant he wasn't looking at us any more. "Whatever you're planning, now would be good," I whispered to Little Ben.

He nodded and began wriggling in his ropes.

"You're not going to slip out of them," I whispered. "They're too tight."

"I'm not trying to slip out," he whispered back. "I'm trying to reach ... this." He managed to stick his face below the collar of his shirt, and using his chin, he pulled something out.

It was the long stick with the grabber claws at the end that he had used to get me a blanket when we first met.

He glanced up at Sirion, but the unicorn was still watching Lady Roslyn, who in turn was too caught up in the momentum of her ceremony to notice us. "I summon you, Albert Edward, Prince of Wales!" she called, and the glowing light, and the ornate paintwork, spread to a third engine off in the corner.

Slowly at first, and then as fast as the others, it added its hissing, rattling voice to the chorus: *HSSSSS. Kchick chick chick. HSSSSS. Kchick chick chick.*

Using the grabber clutched under his chin, Little Ben had loosened the knots around my wrist, but not enough for me to escape. He kept working on them.

Now that all four engines were churning, the puffing clouds of steam began to contract, narrowing into tight columns, like bridges made out of smoke, stretching from each machine to the other, growing ever brighter and denser.

The ropes dropped off my wrist. I stumbled forwards and bent down to untie Little Ben, but he shook his head. "I'll untie myself," he whispered. "Get to your mother before it's too late."

I ran for the steps.

As the hissing and *kchic*king reached a crescendo, the beams of light and smoke changed direction, so that instead of connecting the machines with each other, they were pointing at the centre of the building – exactly at the spot where Lady Roslyn was kneeling. The glowing steam poured into her, and she rose to her feet, and then kept rising, hovering in mid-air.

She, too, began to glow.

Sirion was still staring at her, fascinated, and I hoped his poor hearing would mean he wouldn't notice my footsteps. Unfortunately, when you run on a metal floor, you don't just make noise – you make vibrations, too. He felt them through his hooves and snapped to attention. As I reached the steps, he whinnied angrily and galloped after me.

Up on the mezzanine above, JB heard me, too. He came running down the steps, trapping me in the middle.

To manage the steps, he had turned forwards, pointing his eyes away from me. I kept running up the steps, right towards him, and just at the last minute, I knelt, letting him trip over me. As he tumbled down, right into Sirion, I could hear angry curses and whinnies, but I didn't stop to look.

Up on the second floor, I made it to where Mom was strapped down. I tried to lift the drill, but it was still too heavy.

"Untie my other arm, honey," Mom said. "Maybe I can help."

I looked over at the steps. Sirion and JB had gotten to their feet and were on their way back up.

Frantically, I worked Mom's knots loose, and with her free arm, she shoved and I shoved. The drill swung up easily.

"Press your shirt against the wound," I told her. As soon as Mom's blood stopped flowing, the whole sound-and-light show down on the ground floor came to a sudden stop, with only the glow around Lady Roslyn remaining. She dropped to the floor with a tremendous *clang* – it was like being full of magic made her heavier. She lay there, moaning, looking confused, probably because I had interrupted the charging process.

JB and Sirion made it to the top of the steps. JB looked at me, then down at the moaning Lady Roslyn. He reached a decision. "I'll be back for you in a moment, girlie," he said. He headed back down, while Sirion stood guarding the top of the steps.

Mom, meanwhile, looked pale. "I feel dizzy," she said.

"You've lost blood," I told her, and looked at her wound. Fortunately, it was small enough that the shirt had stopped the bleeding completely. Lady Roslyn had been careful with the Fire Hook.

I needed to get us out of there. But I couldn't exactly fight my way out with sheer physical force. I was going to need more information. "Mom," I said. "Why is this happening to us?"

"I wish I knew, sweetie."

"Is there anything unusual about our family? Did Grandma ever say anything about magical powers?"

Mom squinched up her forehead, the way she always did when she was trying to remember something. "Back when we all moved to America, she said ... what was it? Oh! I remember! She said, 'Our family has long been the servant of one of the most powerful and beneficent magical forces in the world, and that force is intimately associated with London's hidden rivers, but now we must journey to a distant land for complex reasons you will one day understand.' Or, you know, something like that."

I stared at her in disbelief. "And you never mentioned that to me? You told me every single one of Grandma's nine billion sayings about the best way to brush your teeth, but you never thought to mention the whole powerful magical force thing?"

"Well, sweetie, it wasn't in rhyme. That made it much harder to remember."

Down below, Lady Roslyn was beginning to come to her senses. Unfortunately, that was the exact moment that Little Ben managed to get his own knots untied. He took a step forwards, and Lady Roslyn heard his footstep.

She whirled around and pointed a single finger at him. The glow that surrounded her entire body surged for a moment, then focused down to an incredibly bright light on the tip of her finger. A ball of something eye-woundingly bright shot out, straight into Little Ben's chest. He flew backwards, slamming into a wall.

Crap. Maybe I had freed my mom before Lady Roslyn could be fully charged, but she obviously had plenty of power to work with.

Which was terrifying, but it also gave me an idea.

Once, when I was little, Aunt Rainey came over to our house to babysit while Mom went out on some errand. Somehow, Aunt Rainey got started on how amazing the little socket in the wall was. She told me it was full of something called electricity, which was a wonderful force that made modern life possible, and it could move through metal objects, like that fork on the table over there. That would have been fine if it weren't for two things:

1. She forgot to mention that electricity was dangerous, and
2. Right after our conversation, she went off to the kitchen to get a snack, leaving four-year-old me alone with a metal fork and the wonderful, life-giving electrical outlet.

Fortunately, she came back into the room moments before I stuck the fork in the socket, and her terrified scream stopped me from doing it, so I didn't die.

Even so, Aunt Rainey had felt really bad, and she had tried to make up for it by teaching me everything she knew about electricity. The way she explained it, she'd nearly killed me, so she wanted to give me information that could one day save my life.

Of course, I was four, so most of it went over my head. But one thing had stuck with me:

Lightning rods.

Lightning rods, Aunt Rainey told me, were made of iron, and iron conducted electricity. That meant they steered dangerous forces away from people, right down into the ground.

So as I stood on the cast-iron mezzanine of the Crossness Pumping Station, I took out the wire that Inspector Sands had given me and I wrapped one end around my chest. Then I took the other end and tied it to one of the little iron curlicues that decorated the iron floor of this humungous iron building.

I had no idea if it would work, but Inspector Sands had told me that the wire would transmit magic as easily as it would have transmitted electricity. So wouldn't the whole building work the same way?

I didn't want to think about what would happen if it didn't, but I didn't have much choice.

I took a deep breath. I swallowed. I got my courage up as much as I could and yelled down over the mezzanine. "Hey! Roz! I just freed my mom and we're taking our blood home with us. See ya later, lady!"

Lady Roslyn cocked her head, as if choosing from among a dozen sarcastic retorts. Then she just shrugged and pointed.

Unimaginable magical power poured out of her finger, straight at me.

CHAPTER 35

The power streamed into my chest, my skin tingled, and my hair stood up straight, and my eyes watered ...

... but I didn't go flying backwards. It didn't even hurt.

The magic flowed into the wire, circled around my torso, and plunged down. For a moment, I could see it rippling through the floor, and then down through the columns to the level below, before it vanished.

The beam of light faded out. I stood there, un-harmed, grinning.

"How interesting," Lady Roslyn said, and for once, she didn't sound sarcastic. "I have no idea how you managed that."

When she realized I wasn't going to answer that

one, Lady Roslyn shrugged and pointed her finger at me again.

Nothing came out of it. "Out of power," she tsked. "This is what comes of half measures. Hyacinth, I'm truly sorry, but I think I'm going to have to slit your mother's throat after all." She nodded at JB and Sirion.

If my little trick with Inspector Sands's wire had worked, all that magical power had flowed down into the ground, and he and his Saltpetre Men would be on the way. But I had no idea how long it would take them to get here. In the meantime, if I couldn't get Mom away outright, I'd have to keep us both alive as long as I could.

I looked around frantically, left, right, up, down … and then I saw it. Hanging from the ceiling were a bunch of chains on pulleys. I guessed they must have been for lifting up fuel or equipment, back when the pumping station was in operation. Some of them were still connected to heavy cauldrons lying on the floor or up in the rafters. And the end of one of them was lying curled up a few feet away from us.

"Mom," I whispered. "Do exactly what I do."

"OK, dear, but what—"

Before she finished, I ran forwards and grabbed the chain. Mom did exactly what I asked her, which made it twice in an hour – possibly the most amazing thing that had happened so far. Anyway, she ran after me and grabbed the chain, too.

"Jump!" I yelled, and, still holding tight to the chain, I hopped over the edge of the mezzanine. Mom followed me.

As we swung down, desperately clutching the chain, I could see the big cauldron on its other end being lifted up into the air. Fortunately, the cauldron was just a little lighter than Mom and me combined, so our speed was slow enough to give me a little control. I kicked my legs, swinging us towards a stairwell that led down into a faintly glowing darkness. I didn't know what was down there, but as long as it didn't want to cut Mom's throat, I was willing to deal with it.

Hanging on for dear life, we rode the chain down through the stairwell and landed on a shaky iron crosswalk in a small, cramped basement. In each of the four corners of the basement was a big steel tube. Those must have been the furnaces that, under normal circumstances, would have powered the giant machines on the ground floor. But these weren't normal circumstances, and the power was coming from somewhere else. In the middle of the room was a rough dirt pit, and sitting in the pit was the baker's oven that had started the Great Fire. Beams of light shot out from it into the furnaces, pulsing in time with the *HSSSS. Kchick chick chick* from above.

I took a deep breath, expecting to inhale the oven's delicious aroma of fresh bread, but I smelled something thick and metallic instead: blood. In fact, based on the red stains in the iron above it, the oven was in exactly the right spot to catch Mom's dripping blood in its chimney. Even though she was now safely next to me, I shuddered.

I didn't have too much time to think about it, though. There were pipes sticking out of the wall. As we stood there, they convulsed and clanked, and water began to pour out of them.

"I suppose this is appropriate, Hyacinth," Lady Roslyn said, speaking loudly over the sound of the water. I looked up to see her standing at the top of the stairs. "Our little adventure together began when you turned on a small tap, and it just ended with me turning on several rather large ones. You and your mother will both drown within minutes. Alternatively, Mrs Hayward, you can give yourself up of your own free will, and I'll shut off the water, and your daughter and her friends can leave, free and unharmed."

"Oh, I'm Ms Herkanopoulos now," Mom said, trying to sound brave. "I've gone back to my maiden name. And if you'll let them go, then, yes, I'll—"

"Mom, don't. Lady Roslyn is bluffing. She won't drown us. She needs your blood – and the baker's oven – and—"

"I do indeed," Lady Roslyn said. "But I can get blood from a drowned body nearly as easily as a living one. And as for the baker's oven – well, if there's one thing you ought to have learned from our time together, it's that magic works just fine when it's wet."

I looked around wildly for a way out. I couldn't find one. Lady Roslyn was blocking the only exit, and the dirt pit in the middle of the room was already entirely underwater. We didn't have much time.

Mom turned to me. "If I go with her, will she really let you go? Do you think she'll keep her word?"

I *knew* Lady Roslyn would keep her word. She couldn't risk lying with so much magic around. Neither could I, but I couldn't tell Mom the truth, either, because then she'd just sacrifice herself like a big dummy and everything I had done to rescue her would be for nothing.

So I just stood there, not saying anything. I guess Mom knew me pretty well, because my silence was all the answer she needed. "I'll do it," she said to Lady Roslyn.

"No!" I yelled as Mom started up the staircase. I grabbed her arm and held it tight, but she shook her head.

"Sweetie, look down," she said. I looked down. The water was already rising above my ankles. I hadn't even felt it – all I could feel was how terrified I was for my mother. "I'm going to die either way," Mom said. "At least let me go knowing I saved you. Please, let me go."

I looked in her eyes, and I knew what I had just heard: it was my mom's dying wish.

Even so, I didn't want to let go. I didn't want to *ever* let go. But I must have, because the next thing I knew, Mom was climbing up the stairs, and I was just standing there, my hand outstretched, tears running down my face.

CHAPTER 36

$\mathcal{T}$he water at my feet began to bubble.

For an instant, I thought it was my imagination, or just the tears making everything blurry. But, no, there was something different about the water. It was seething as though something was pushing up from below.

Something grey and muddy and shaped like a head.

Like a grey, muddy head with a dark red streak and glittering mica eyes.

A Saltpetre Man rose out of the water, and was joined by another, and another, and another, the clay of their bodies wet and glistening. For the first time ever, they looked absolutely beautiful to me. And soon there were more and more and more, filling the whole room.

"Mom!" I yelled. "Stop! It's the Saltpetre Men!"

Mom turned around and looked. Her mouth dropped open.

I guess if I had thought about it, I would have realized that she wouldn't be thrilled by the sudden appearance of the giant dirt monsters that had kidnapped her before. But it didn't even occur to me until Mom turned pale and let out a horrified shriek.

"It's OK," I said. "They're—"

Screaming, Mom turned around and ran the rest of the way up the steps. As she passed JB, he grabbed her and bundled her out of sight. Lady Roslyn gazed down at me with a disturbingly confident look on her face, then turned around and followed JB.

By now, dozens of Saltpetre Men were clomping their way up the steps. "Let me by!" I called, trying to push my way through, but they were too big to pass and too heavy to shove out of the way. All I could do was climb slowly behind them, step by agonizing step.

A hand touched my shoulder. I turned around to see Inspector Sands. "We have the building ssurrounded, Hyassinth. You and your mother are ssafe."

I wanted to believe him. But if he was right, why hadn't Lady Roslyn looked more worried?

Finally, we reached the top. The platoon of Saltpetre Men parted respectfully for Inspector Sands, revealing

Lady Roslyn, JB, and Sirion, backed up against a wall. They had tied Mom to one of the columns.

Lady Roslyn had a chain in her hands and that same confident look on her face. "Inspector Sands," she said. "I thought you might come, and this time, I am prepared. No more mucking about in a kitchen cabinet."

While she was talking, I traced the chain upwards with my eyes. It went all the way up to the ceiling, where it ran through a pulley, then split into a half dozen other chains. And each of those chains was connected to a metal cauldron hanging from the ceiling.

Suddenly, I realized what must be in those cauldrons. "Inspector Sands! Get your men out of—" I began, but it was too late.

Lady Roslyn pulled the chain.

The cauldrons tipped over, and clear liquid came gushing out of them. It smashed down into the mezzanine, poured through the holes in the iron floor, and drenched the army of Saltpetre Men shuffling towards Lady Roslyn.

The flood dissolved them, like chalk marks being rinsed off a blackboard.

Because Inspector Sands wore an officer's cap, he had a tiny bit more protection than the others. That, plus his faster shuffle, gave him just enough time to duck under a wooden table. But as the flood of liquid skittered across the floor, it sploshed up over his shoes, dissolving his ankles. Detached from his feet, his legs collapsed into the flood, dissolving further. By the time the liquid had drained away, there was nothing left of him below the waist.

I had thrown my hands up as the wave crashed towards me. It hadn't helped: I was soaked. But I was totally unharmed, if a little sticky.

"Saltpetre is a chemical substance, and all chemical substances can be dissolved by something," Lady Roslyn explained cheerfully. "Ammonia will do it, but it's awfully nasty. Fortunately, glycerine works just as well. They use it in food all the time – it's totally harmless. To humans, at least."

Inspector Sands looked around. His men were nothing more than a field of empty uniforms and scattered mica chips that had once been eyes. He looked up at the ceiling, then down at the basement, and then he stared intensely at Lady Roslyn, as if he was wondering how it had all gone so wrong.

Then, with his hands, he dragged himself up to one of the building's iron columns and started banging his head against it, over and over.

HSSSSSSS. *Kchick chick chick* went the steam pumps. *CLANG* went Inspector Sands's head.

It was the saddest, most hopeless song I'd ever heard, and it only got worse when Lady Roslyn started to cackle.

HSSSSSSS. Kchick chick chick. CLANG. *"Hee hee hee!"*

When she had stopped laughing, she turned to me, beaming. "It's over, Hyacinth," she said. "I've won."

CHAPTER 37

"*W*ell, you know, there's winning, and then there's *winning*," said a familiar voice, and Newfangled Troy strode in through the entryway. I felt a surge of hope, until I remembered that the last time I had seen him, he had sold me off to the highest bidder.

He had something in his hand, which he was casually throwing in the air. As he stepped forwards into the light, I saw that it looked a little bit like a hammer, and a little bit like a wrench, and a little bit like a saw.

Lady Roslyn gasped. "Bazalgette's Trowel," she hissed. Then she got control of herself and said, more casually, "What makes you think I'd be interested in it?"

Troy shrugged. "Oh, not much. Just *everything*.

I was sitting around at home, looking back on my many adventures, and I started wondering how the Trowel ended up in Hyacinth's hands. Then I remembered something. You were involved in an incident at the mouth of the Tyburn, which ended up in a lot of dead toshers. And that happens to be the same place the Trowel was first discovered, a century ago. Magical things have a way of returning to their sources, so maybe the Trowel ended up back there recently. And maybe you found out about it, and maybe you let a bunch of toshers die so that you could find it."

"And why would I go through so much trouble?" Lady Roslyn asked.

"I work a lot of jobs," Troy said, "which means I hear all sorts of office gossip. I hear things from barbers and carpenters and grocery clerks. Oh, and plumbers. Like the plumber who got an awfully nice fee from an old lady, on the condition that he leave a strange-looking tool in a young girl's bathroom."

"*You* hired that plumber?" I asked Lady Roslyn. And then I figured it out. "It's my bloodline again, isn't it? My family has powers that yours doesn't. Your plan to take over the magical rivers began with a single magically charged drop of water – but you needed somebody from my family to charge it up in the first place. So you left Bazalgette's Trowel for me. But how could you know I'd use it on the sink?"

"You're making a lot of assumptions that—" She stopped and gave her head a little shake. "At this point, there's no need for going round the glasshouse, is there? I can give you a few direct answers before you die. So: I couldn't be sure you'd use Bazalgette's Trowel on the sink," Lady Roslyn said. "But it was worth a try. Do you know how many years I lived in that ugly little building, just so I could be close to a member of your family when they finally moved back? No matter how I tried, I never managed to trick your aunt into helping me out. But you, my dear, proved a much easier mark."

"A nice little con," Troy said cheerfully. "I tip my hat to you. But once you had the drop, you took your eye off the Trowel. And without it, any power you take on is going to get used up, eventually. Of course, if you had the very piece of kit that Mr Bazalgette used to seal the power of the rivers under the ground, you could seal the power within yourself. Nothing could ever take it away from you, could it?"

"Troy, no!" I yelled.

They both ignored me. Lady Roslyn licked her lips. "And what is it you want in exchange?"

"Oh, nothing much. One million pounds would do it."

"Ah, I see," Lady Roslyn said. "You've noticed that

elderly ladies keep all sorts of loose change in their purses, and so you quite reasonably assume I've got fifty million tuppence clattering around mine. Unfortunately, I seem to have left my purse at home."

"Give me your word that you'll pay me within seven days, and I'll place Bazalgette's Trowel in your hands right now."

Lady Roslyn was not impressed. "Carefully phrased, young man. You'll *place it in my hands*. That's not the same thing as making me the owner of it. And using a tosheroon of such power could be most hazardous to my health, if it doesn't recognize me as its owner."

And just like that, I saw how I was going to get us out of this mess. I was going to have to phrase my next sentence very, very carefully, though. I wished Inspector Sands would stop banging his head. Somehow, even with all the other noise, it was that sad, desperate clanging that made it hard to think. *Focus, Hyacinth.*

I cleared my throat. "Troy can't give you ownership if he doesn't own it, can he? I'm the one who found it in the first place. Remember? That's what started this whole thing. And I'm willing to transfer all my ownership to you, for a price of my own."

Troy must have known what I was up to, since he gave me a discreet wink.

"A price?" said Lady Roslyn. "I suppose you want *two* million pounds?"

"No. Let me and my mom go."

"The Trowel's no use without your mother, I'm afraid."

I knew she'd say that, but I also knew she'd be suspicious if I didn't ask for enough. Fortunately, Mom helped out by saying, "Save yourself, sweetie. Promise me you will."

I pretended to think about it for a moment. "I promise, Mom. I'll save myself," I said. This was true. If my plan worked, I'd be saving myself ... as well as her. I tried to look dejected as I told Lady Roslyn, "Do what you need to do. But let me and Oaroboarus and Little Ben go."

Lady Roslyn nodded. "You have yourself a deal." She nodded to Troy. "And you? All I need from you is the Trowel, not ownership of it. I'll give you a hundred pounds. Or I can have JB kill you, and then I'll take the Trowel for free."

"Can't say fairer than that," Troy said, and threw her the Trowel.

She snatched it from the air and looked expectantly at me. "Let's hear it, Hyacinth. And don't try to get cute with the phrasing, or the deal's off."

"OK," I said. "I hereby give you every single bit of

ownership I have in Bazalgette's Trowel."

While Lady Roslyn thought that over, I prayed she wouldn't notice the loophole. I had given her all the ownership I had – it's just, that happened to be zilch. After all, I had given Troy all rights to the Trowel, back in the collapsing underground church. Troy and I knew that, but Lady Roslyn didn't … I hoped.

Finally, she nodded. "That is acceptable. You may go."

"No. I want to stay and keep Mom company while… Anyway, I want to stay."

She shrugged. "As you wish. JB, keep an eye on her. Make sure she stays precisely where she is."

"Good luck to all of you," Troy said. He winked at me again, then strode off through the archway, whistling as he left.

A bit of movement up on the mezzanine caught my attention. Little Ben had apparently woken up and made his way to where Oaroboarus was lying. Quickly, I cast my eyes back down. If JB or Lady Roslyn noticed where I was looking, they'd spot Little Ben. And if I was right that Oaroboarus was still alive, and Little Ben could get him free without being discovered, I would have a big stubborn ace up my sleeve.

Lady Roslyn lifted Bazalgette's Trowel and pointed

it at each of the steam engines in turn. "Queen Victoria, I summon your power! Prince Consort, I summon your power! Edward Albert, Prince of Wales, I summon your power! Alexandra, Princess of Wales, I summon your power!"

She held the sharp edge of the Trowel against my mother's neck, as if choosing where she was going to cut. I started forwards, but JB moved menacingly between me and Mom.

"Mighty engines, as full and rightful owner of Bazalgette's Trowel, I seal your power within me!" Lady Roslyn cried, and swung her arm back, ready to slash Mom's neck –

– and then she paused and cocked her head, as if she had just heard something strange.

I heard it, too. There was a wrong note in the industrial symphony that filled the building. Inspector Sands's head still beat a clanging percussion against the iron column, but the steam section of the orchestra was playing a slightly different tune. *Clang. HSSSS. Kchicka chick CHUNK.*

Once again, beams of glowing steam shot out of the mighty engines.

Clang. HSSSS. Kchicka chick CHUNK.

The beams hunted across the room like spotlights from a guard tower, finally converging on the Trowel.

Clang. HSSSS. Kchicka chick CHUNK CHUNK CHUNK.

Realization dawned on Lady Roslyn's face. She tried to drop the Trowel. Her fingers wouldn't budge.

Clang. HSSSS. Kchicka chick CHUNK CHUNK CHUNK CHUNK CHUNK CHUNK.

She reached up with her other hand, trying to pry her fingers off, but they wouldn't let go. The Trowel grew bright, and then grew brighter. I could barely stand to look at it.

Clang. HSSSS. Kchicka chick CHUNK CHUNK CHUNK CHUNK CHUNK CHUNK CHUNK CHUNK CHUNK CHUNK CHUNK CHUNK.

The Trowel trembled upwards, forcing Lady Roslyn to stand on her tiptoes. It rose higher still, dragging her with it, until she was floating as high as the mezzanine, and that loud, wrong, pounding noise drowned out all the other sounds. CHUNK CHUNK CHUNK CHUNK CHUNK CHUNK. She floated higher still, until the Trowel met the ceiling. CHUNK CHUNK CHUNK CHUNK CHUNK CHUNK. It was shaking violently now, wrenching Lady Roslyn back and forth, and the CHUNK CHUNK CHUNK grew louder as the Trowel shook more and more CHUNK CHUNK CHUNK violently and it CHUNK CHUNK CHUNK grew so bright I had to close my eyes, and CHUNK

CHUNK CHUNK then CHUNK CHUNK CHUNK for CHUNK CHUNK CHUNK one CHUNK CHUNK CHUNK sweet CHUNK CHUNK CHUNK moment –

– there was almost total silence. The steam engines stopped moving. The Trowel stopped shaking. Only the *clang* of Inspector Sands's head disturbed the quiet.

I opened my eyes a crack, and then opened them wide and gasped. The glowing cloud had split into a hundred angry faces that billowed around the Trowel in a furious swarm. They were, I realized, the spirits that Lady Roslyn had summoned, and they were not happy.

For a moment, they pulled back.

Then they shot forwards, vanishing into the Trowel.

And in that instant, the Trowel exploded with a colossal roar.

I caught a glimpse of Lady Roslyn plummeting towards the ground, and of metal and wood fragments shooting towards me, and then it was blocked out by a massive shadow. As the shadow passed, I realized it was Oaroboarus, leaping down from the mezzanine just in time to shield me.

I looked around. Mom, thank heavens, had been shielded by the iron column she was tied to. Sirion and

JB weren't so lucky – they were lying unconscious on the ground looking bruised, with large lumps of steel lying nearby.

Oaroboarus, too, was unconscious once again. His side was covered with shallow welts where the fragments had hit him, but nothing had penetrated too deeply into his thick, bristly hide. He was going to be fine.

We've won, I thought.

And that's when Lady Roslyn came running at me, a crazed look in her eye, wielding a long, sharp fragment of the Trowel as if it were a knife.

CHAPTER 38

She dove at me, blade held high, and knocked me to the ground. As her hand slashed down towards my neck, I grabbed her arm. Getting sucked up to the ceiling and then exploded down to the floor must have worn her out, because I was able to hold her arm a full two inches away from my neck.

"You promised you'd let me go," I told her as I pushed with all my might. "Remember the whole can't-break-your-word-around-magic rule? Hello?"

She didn't answer except to snarl, completely incoherent with fury. OK. Looked like I wasn't going to be able to reason with her. On the plus side, if she succeeded in killing me, thereby breaking her word, she'd probably get squashed when the building collapsed.

That was kind of a consolation.

I couldn't consider it too deeply, though, since I was focusing all my energy on keeping a razor-sharp piece of steel out of my throat. Even in her weakened state, I couldn't move her arm any farther away. In fact, I must have been even more exhausted than she was, because the blade was creeping closer and closer.

I guess this is it, I thought. *Great. The last thing I'm ever going to see is Lady Roslyn, and the last thing I'm ever going to hear is Inspector Sands's head going* clang. *Or maybe* clung.

Wait. *Clung?* Why had the sound changed? Taking my eyes off the blade for just a moment, I stole a glance in Inspector Sands's direction. He was still pounding his head against the iron column ... but now the column was beginning to bend the teeniest bit.

Clung. It bent more. Much more. As it happened, it was one of the columns that held up the mezzanine, and now that Inspector Sands had weakened it, the weight of the mezzanine began to bend it even more. He hadn't been banging his head out of despair – he had been trying to bring down the building.

Clung. The mezzanine tilted visibly.

Clung. The column snapped in half.

The mezzanine dropped.

Everything that had been on the mezzanine began to slide downwards:

Scattered tools.

Bits of metal.

Long, heavy chains.

Little Ben, who grabbed on to a railing and held tight.

Oh, and the giant industrial drill began to slide downwards, too, sending sparks flying everywhere as it scraped along the floor.

In about two seconds, that drill was going to crash down on exactly the spot where Lady Roslyn and I were wrestling.

Time for a massive gamble. I let go of Lady Roslyn's arm for a moment. Since she was putting all her weight into pushing down on me, she toppled. Moments before the knife hit my throat, I used every last bit of strength I had and pushed her legs up with my knees, flipping her up in the air –

and I rolled out from under her –

– the blade went soaring through the air –

– and by now the mezzanine was completely vertical –

– and Little Ben lost his grip on the railing, crashing down to the ground –

– and the drill tumbled down, too, dropping though the air –

– right onto Lady Roslyn's foot, pinning her to the iron floor. She screamed in pain, but she was trapped.

I pulled myself to my feet and looked over to where Mom was tied up. Little Ben had landed next to her. He staggered to his feet.

He looked at Mom, then at the steel blade, lying nearby on the ground.

He picked it up. He lifted the blade high.

My stomach twisted in sudden fear. *Was he evil after all?*

I stumbled towards them, but before I could reach them, he brought the blade down –

– and cut the ropes tying Mom to the pillar.

"Thank you, small person I don't recognize," Mom said to him.

"My pleasure, mother of my friend!" he said cheerfully. He dropped the blade and went over to try to wake Oaroboarus.

Mom and I stood a moment looking at each other.

Then we fell into each other's arms, crying. I hugged my mother tight, and for a long time.

CHAPTER 39

*W*hen Mom and I finally let each other go, Inspector Sands, still lying on the ground, cleared his throat. "If you would be sso kind, I could usze a new pair of legss. Could you go get ssome mud for me, pleasse?"

"Of course," I said.

By now, Oaroboarus was back on his feet. Inspector Sands gave him a significant look. "We have reczeived exsstenssive complaintss about a giant boar trampling carss. Asz an unlicsenssed magical creature, your pressencze above ground iss forbidden. It iss my duty to arresst you, no matter how heroic you have been today. Alass, asz long asz I have no legss, there iss little I can do to prevent you from esscaping. Hyassinth, pleasse be sspeedy with that mud. If you took, ssay, five minutess, the boar would get too far away, and there would be no point in my purssuing him."

"Message received," I said.

Little Ben and Oaroboarus accompanied me outside.

"I'd better go with Oaroboarus," Little Ben said. "It's time I went back to my dad's files."

So we hugged each other goodbye. I don't want to spoil anybody's reputation for toughness, so I won't go into detail, but I'll tell you one thing. It turned out that giant boars shed absolutely huge tears. It also turned out that Oaroboarus was as stubborn about letting go of a hug as he was about everything else. Finally, I shoved him away.

"If we take any longer, Inspector Sands is going to drag himself out and arrest you, legs or no legs."

Oaroboarus nodded reluctantly.

KINDLY EXCUSE MY

PREMATURE DEPARTURE.

WE SHALL MEET AGAIN.

"Ooh! That's right!" Little Ben said, beaming, "I *know* we will, because Troy said you were the key to me finding my answers, and that hasn't happened yet, so we *have* to meet again."

He climbed up on Oaroboarus's back and waved at me one last time.

"Thank you," I said. "Thank you both for everything."

Oaroboarus nodded, and with a few mighty bounds, he was out of sight.

Back inside, I handed Inspector Sands an armful of mud and watched him shape it into new legs for himself. A thought occurred to me. "When you started banging on that pillar – how could you know it would end up saving my life?"

"I am pleaszed I ssaved you, but that wass not my intention. I ssimply wisshed to break the magzical ssircuit Lady Rossslyn wass ussing, and sssending the drill craszhing down ssseemed the besst way to do sso."

He put the finishing touches on his new toes and stood up. His new legs squelched a bit, but they held his weight.

Then, somehow – I never quite figured out how – he summoned reinforcements. A new squad of Saltpetre Men marched up from the basement and scooped up Sirion and JB. As they lifted the industrial drill off Lady Roslyn's foot, Inspector Sands led Mom and me towards the exit. "I have reported your cooperaszion to my ssupervissor, and szhe hass authorizsed me to releasze you," he said, and gestured to a black cab idling outside.

I ran to it and peered in the window, but the driver was just a driver. I had never seen him before.

Mom and I climbed into the back and rode off. I turned to wave goodbye to Inspector Sands. He saluted, then melted away into the ground.

The cab drove off, and I watched the Crossness Pumping Station fade into the distance.

We had a long drive ahead of us. I used it to tell Mom everything that had happened.

I had just reached the part where Lady Roslyn stole the oven that had started the Great Fire when I realized that the taxi driver was talking, too. We were stopped at a light, waiting to turn right, and he had rolled down his window to chat with another taxi driver.

I looked over at the other cabbie. It was Newfangled Troy.

Quickly as I could, I rolled down my own window. The light in the other direction was turning yellow, and Troy was in the left-hand lane. As soon as the light changed, we'd be heading in opposite directions. We only had a few seconds, and a million questions banged around inside my head.

The one that finally popped out through my mouth was "Whose side are you on?"

"Maybe that depends on who's got the most money," he answered.

"Nice try, but that 'maybe' means you're going around the glasshouse," I said. "And if you just care about money, why didn't you tell Lady Roslyn that you *did* own the Trowel? It would have been worth a million pounds."

He grinned. "I think you're getting the hang of this," he said. "Next time we meet, you'll be the one bailing me out ... maybe."

The light changed, and when he drove off, I had no idea where he was headed.

But I knew where I was going. Mom had been right. As long as she was with me, anywhere I went was home.

ACKNOWLEDGEMENTS

$\mathcal{I}$ started writing this book nearly nine years ago. Along the way, I've been lucky enough to have the help of many kind and generous people. My heartfelt thanks to:

Matthew David Brozik, Kristin Grey, Miriam Halahmy, Teme Ring, Emily Rosenbaum, Simon Rosenbaum, Courtney Rubin, and Kate Strauss, who offered feedback and encouragement on early drafts;

My agent, Ammi-Joan Paquette;

My editors, Diane Landolf at Random House and Gill Evans at Walker UK, as well as the entire teams at both houses;

All my children's teachers and caregivers, especially Laura and Lore;

My whole family, especially my wife, Lauren, and our children.

AUTHOR'S NOTE

$\mathcal{I}$ made up much less of this book than you might think.

There really are a number of lost rivers flowing beneath the streets of London. If you know where to look, you can see the ones that haven't been diverted into the sewers emptying out into the river Thames. Or you can go to the Sloane Square station on the Underground and when you're standing on the platform, look up. The big metal tube over your head carries the river Westbourne.

This shows the river Westbourne aqueduct over Sloane Square station in the 1920s.

There really is a monument in the parking lot of Charing Cross station that looks like the very tip of a giant underground cathedral. It's actually a Victorian replica of a thirteenth century memorial that King Edward I put up in memory of his wife, Eleanor. (Of course, that's just what I'd say if I wanted to help keep the giant underground cathedral a secret, isn't it?)

The Mount Pleasant Mail Sorting Facility is a real Royal Mail facility. It's built on the former spot of the Coldbath Fields Prison, and prisoners there were forced to walk on a treadmill as a form of punishment. The treadmills aren't there any more – but by the time this book is published, a new Postal Museum

at Mount Pleasant should be open for visitors.

The Monument to the Great Fire of London really is 202 feet tall, and it really does stand 202 feet from where the Great Fire of London began. You can visit it and climb to the top most days of the year. Personally, I've never seen it topple over onto its side, but maybe you'll be luckier than I've been. Directions and opening hours are at themonument.info

A close-up reveals the birdcage-like railing that forms a roof over visitors.

The Monument

Unless you have a magical umbrella to carry and a magical tune to whistle, you can't get access to most of London's sewer system. But you can visit the Crossness Pumping Station once a year during Open House London, which takes place on a weekend in September. Visit openhouselondon.org.uk for more information.

Inside the Crossness Pumping Station

$\mathcal{J}$acob Sager Weinstein has written for the *New Yorker*, *McSweeney's*, HBO and the BBC. He lives in London with his family, close to where the Westbourne flows underground, but his sink mixes hot and cold water nonetheless. He apologizes in advance for any Great Fires this may cause. Visit him at www.jacobsagerweinstein.com, or follow him on Twitter: @jacobsw.

GET RUMBLING WITH THE ROMANS!

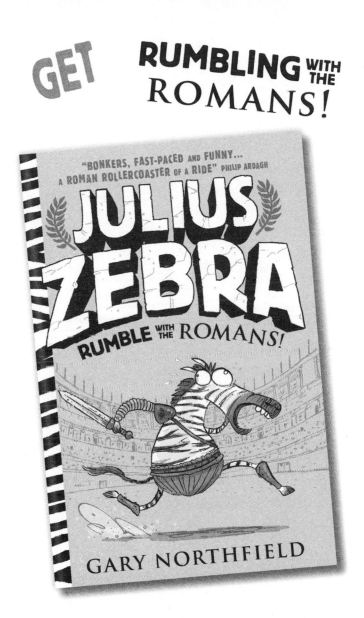

"BONKERS, FAST-PACED AND FUNNY... A ROMAN ROLLERCOASTER OF A RIDE" PHILIP ARDAGH

JULIUS ZEBRA

RUMBLE WITH THE ROMANS!

GARY NORTHFIELD

THEN ENJOY...

BUNDLING WITH THE BRITONS

"STUPID, CLEVER AND VERY VERY FUNNY"
JIM SMITH, CREATOR OF
BARRY LOSER

BUT... BEWARE OF GETTING

ENTANGLED WITH THE EGYPTIANS!

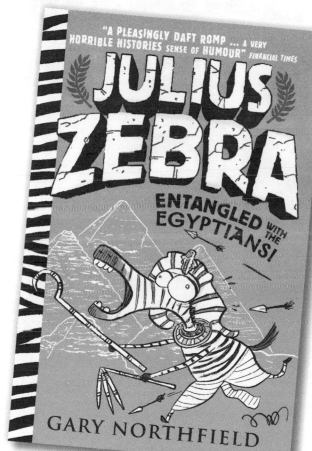

COMING SOON!

"Forget the summer holidays, forget your birthday, and forget Christmas, I can guarantee that this is what you've been waiting for." Sam, aged 11, Lovereading4kids.co.uk